CW01646401

T

He-Witch

Further adventures of Micah Judd

as set down by

Jack Elwin

First published in 2006

Published by Firkin Publications,
4 Portesham Hill, Portesham, Weymouth, Dorset

Printed by the County Products Press
DT2 8LL

Copyright © Jack Elwin 2006

The moral right of the author has been asserted.

All rights reserved.
No part of this publication may be reproduced, stored in a retrieval system, or transmitted, in any form or by any means, without the prior permission in writing of the publisher, nor be otherwise circulated in any form of binding or cover other than that in which it is published and without a similar condition including this condition being imposed on the subsequent purchaser.

ISBN 0-9551633-1-5

* * * * * * * * * * *

Other Micah Judd stories by Jack Elwin:
Three Treasures
Powder and Plots

Chapter 1 A He-witch

ONE DOESN'T EXPECT to meet a mob howling for blood on a sunny Thursday morning.

I was standing in South Street, talking to my friend, Mr Lawrence Huatt the pewterer. Dorchester that morning towards the latter part of May, in the year of our Lord 1644, was as busy, noisy and smelly as usual. Straw and horse-droppings littered the road, but as it had not rained lately my shoes were not much soiled. Shop-keepers and hawkers were crying their wares, while dogs and children darted in and out amongst the people who were chaffering for goods or, like us, simply standing to gossip.

'Do you think it would be safe to travel to Poole?' Lawrence wondered. 'I need to see a fellow of my trade there, and collect some pieces of scrap he has put by for me. Now Prince Maurice and his ruffians have moved westwards, the way to Poole should be quiet, do you think?'

Prince Maurice, who had allowed his troops to rampage through Dorchester when he came here the previous August, and had gone on to capture Weymouth and Portland Castle, had been besieging Lyme for over a month. We who inclined to the Parliamentary side had been both shamed and encouraged by the gallant resistance of the people there, so much more steadfast than our own.

'I wouldn't be too sure of that,' I replied. 'There may still be marauding soldiers about, beside bands of deserters turned to highway robbery.'

'The Lord forfend, Micah, for I can't delay much longer. I shall have to trust the Lord for his protection and abide under the shadow of the Almighty.'

Lawrence Huatt has always larded his speech with scriptural words, which make him honoured among the godly of the town.

'I wouldn't, Lawrence, not for a while. For although (by the last we heard) Poole was still firmly in Parliament's hands, remember that Wareham has been betrayed to the Cavaliers. If you weren't robbed by the one side you almost certainly would be by the other. No, Lawrence, I wouldn't go travelling in that direction—or any direction, for that matter—until things are more settled.'

'But when will that be?' he asked. 'Last year we were saying that the war would be over in a few months—we thought it would pass us by—and just think of the losses we've had since then and the state we're in now!'

I could only agree, although thanks to my efforts (and a lot of luck) Lawrence's losses weren't nearly as great as they might have been. I was about to remind him of the fact, when we heard an increase in the general noise and paused in our talk to look. There was some disturbance going on at the far end of the street, a noise which was drawing nearer. Soon we could hear the creak and rattle of a cart and the yells and catcalls of a mob surrounding it. Everyone about us also paused to turn and stare. The idlers and urchins in the street began darting and weaving past more sober townspeople, pressing towards the disturbance to add their shouts to those of the mob. I could see arms and cudgels being waved in the air, and there was a sort of wild chant, which as they drew nearer resolved into 'Burn him! Burn him!'

As the cart drew nearer I saw that it was being guarded by four mounted soldiers led by a young officer, a Cornet perhaps. They were Cavaliers no doubt, for since Prince Maurice's victories of the past months the King's forces were now in control of most of Dorset. The soldiers had their swords drawn and were keeping the mob from getting too close to the cart, which was pulled by a pair of oxen and driven by a grubby gloomy-looking man with a shapeless brown hat on his head. Lying in the cart was a poor fellow with long grey hair, looking like a wild man of the woods, with his hands tied together, as were also his ankles which stuck out at the back of the cart. He looked as if he had been slung into the cart like a sack and had stayed slumped in a heap.

The mob swirled about us, angry men and youths and even quite a lot of women. I could feel their heat and smell the sweat of their bodies and was almost overcome by the fervour of their fury and fear, as they kept shouting, 'Burn him! Burn the witch!' Lawrence and I drew back as far as we could to allow them to pass, pushed this way and that as too many people tried get by all at once. Here came the cart creaking and rattling over the cobbles, and the noise of the mob became almost unbearable as it went past.

I stared at the prisoner and exclaimed:

'Heaven help us! that's Malachy Moore!'

'Who? the prisoner?' asked Mr Huatt. 'Do you know him?'

'I do indeed,' I said. 'At least, I don't know much about him, but I have met him, and he was of great service to me. He's known as the Wise Man of Upwey.'

'He doesn't look very wise at present,' said Huatt. Certainly Malachy was in a bad way. His face was swollen and there was blood on his cheek and one eye was puffy and closed. He looked as if he had been in a fight.

As the crowd passed and the noise lessened a little, I grabbed the arm of a youth who was near the back bobbing up and down trying to see over the heads of those in front.

'What's going on?' I asked.

''Tis a witch,' he said. 'We was goin' to duck him, but the so'jers stopped us.'

'A witch?' said Huatt. 'Do you mean a wizard?'

'He-witch, wizard—makes no difference,' said the youth as he broke free and ran after the others to join in the shouting, 'Burn him! burn him!'

'Whatever have they done to poor old Malachy?' I said, craning to see over the backs of the mob.

'I shall keep well away from it, and I'd advise you to do so too,' said Lawrence. 'Satan goeth about seeking whom he may devour, and 'tis best to avoid all meddling with him and those who practise his wicked arts.'

'But what if the man's innocent?'

'Then let us hope he may have a proper trial, that in the mouth of two or three witnesses all may be established in due form. But excuse me, Micah—I must be off, I think, for it looks as if this rabble may pass my shop, and I must try to see that they don't do damage. Where are the constables? This is almost a riot.'

'All the same I'm going find out what it's all about,' I said.

'Get back home and see to your shop, is my advice. But there, you'll go your own way, I don't doubt,' he said. 'But take care, for even if you escape taint by the devil you'll be in danger of getting your clothes torn or your pockets picked!'

But I took no heed of him, and followed the crowd, as did many others from the street. The procession turned right into East Street and down the hill and stopped at the new gaol, built about ten years ago. The grey stone walls were beginning to look less new and harsh, but it was still a grim building, threatening doom for evil-doers, and perhaps for those whose luck had run out.

The officer dismounted and hammered on the door with the hilt of his sword and, when after some delay it was opened, exchanged quite a lot of words with the gaol-keeper, though I couldn't hear what was said, then turned and gave an order to his men. One of them dismounted and cut the rope binding the prisoner's ankles and helped him down, while the other soldiers prevented the spectators from coming too close.

'Keep back, if ye want to escape slashing!' one of the soldiers shouted, and they all waved their swords about in a threatening way, so that the people bunched together just out of reach.

Malachy walked stiffly into the gaol, limping a little, and the door was shut with a heavy thud—an ominous sound.

The officer and his man remounted.

'Now, good people,' he raised his voice to the crowd, 'get you home. You have seen the prisoner safely lodged, and the justices will try him in due course. So home with you!'

His men made as if to slash at them, and the officer shouted again, 'Be off with you! Get you to your homes!'

Slowly the crowd began to drift away, though one or two still stood and shouted 'Burn him!' a few more times. I stood my ground until a clear view opened towards the officer, when I called out:

'Sir, by your leave, I know this man you've brought in. Why is he a prisoner? What is he charged with?'

'Murder and witchcraft, or rather (as I understand) murder by witchcraft.'

'But what has he done, sir?'

'I know not. But I saved his life.'

'How is that, sir?'

'We were on patrol as far as Upwey, over the hill there, and found a mob of rioting rapscallions about to throw him into the millpond. I saw the disturbance and thought that murder being done. Had I known they were ducking a witch I would not have interfered. However, having charged among them and ordered them to disperse, we couldn't very well just leave him there, so we saved him from the mob. But if he's going to be burned he might wish that we'd left him to drown!'

'Are you going to lay a charge against him?' I asked.

'Not I,' he replied, 'as I said, I know nothing about him. No doubt some of the Upwey people will bring charges if there's any truth in what they were saying. If none of them come forward I daresay he'll be released when things calm down. At all events I've done my duty, and have no more to do with this affair.'

He was about to ride off when the carter called out:

'Oi, sir, when am I to be paid?'

'Apply to the justices,' said the officer, and he kicked his heels into his horse's flanks and rode off followed by his men.

'Bloody so'jers,' said the carter, 'bloody justices, bloody witchcraft.'

'Are you from Upwey?' I asked him. 'What really happened there?'

'Old Malachy, he went too far this time, that's what. He's been near trouble several times o' late, with his evil eye an' that ol' black puss o' his—if it is a puss and not an evil Incupuss.'

'What did Malachy do?' I asked.

'Put a spell on a gentleman from Melcombe so that he died. Very nasty it were, I believe. They so'jers ought to ha' let 'un be thrown in the water. He'd ha' floated, sure thing, and that would ha' proved that he done it.'

'But how do you know the gentleman's death was due to Malachy?'

'He cussed 'un didn' he? Cussed 'un so he took ill all sudden like, an' sickened an' died. 'Twere a horrible death, by all accounts, a real devilish death. I wouldn' ha' carried the witch in my cart for a hundred pounds if the so'jers hadn' forced me, and God alone knows what evil will ha' rubbed off on it. I'll have to wash it down an' get passon to exorcise it wi' a bit o' his bless'd water. 'Tis a terrible thing, witchcraft, and I be half afeard now to ride my cart home. Maybe if I keep repeating the "Our Father" I'll be all right. Do you think that'll keep the devil off me, sir?'

'I should think so,' I said, 'but why not add the Creed and the Nunc dimittis for good measure?'

My irony was lost upon him, for he said:

'Thank 'ee, sir, you're in the right. So there, I mun be getting along, afore they so'jers take me an' my cart for summat else. I was afeared they wouldn't pay me, nor 'ave they, God rot 'em! But when men have swords and guns 'tis no use arguing—you have to do what they say.'

He shouted at his oxen and lumbered away.

As I walked home to my apothecary's shop up Durn Lane I wondered what, if anything, I ought to do. I had met old Malachy a few months before when he had used a hazel twig to find hidden money that had been stolen by soldiers, as I've described elsewhere in my account of how I recovered the Three Treasures. It was then that I heard he was called 'The Wise Man of Upwey', and I had had the impression then that his neighbours laughed at his strangeness and odd ways, yet feared his powers. When I met him I myself had had some qualms about seeking his aid. His manner, and his piercing eyes, made me fear that he was in touch with ghostly powers better left undisturbed. Yet he had helped me, and (as far as I could tell) had called upon no devils or spirits. In fact, apart from his strangeness, he seemed to be a harmless old man.

As I recalled all this I resolved at least to visit him in the prison, for silly mobs, particularly if they are frightened as well as ignorant, can so easily pick upon some poor wretch, and account him or her guilty of witchcraft without real evidence. Normally the Dorchester folk are kind, but when frightened of the devil or popery they can be do terrible things.

I thought of how not many months ago two priests had been brought out to the old Roman amphitheatre we called Maumbury Rings to face a traitor's punishment. At the last moment one had denied the Pope and sworn loyalty to the King and been spared. But the other, Hugh Green, suffered the full process of being hanged, drawn and quartered. When at last his head was cut off the mob went wild: they caught some Roman Catholics, beat them up, and played football with Green's head. That disgraceful scene took place because so many in the crowd were ignorant and afraid, and the same sort of frenzy (thought I) probably happened in Upwey over Malachy. For witchcraft is a fearful thing, and the devil powerful and frightening.

But if that terrible charge is brought, how can anyone prove his innocence? It is difficult, if not impossible.

I was musing on these things when I turned up Durn Lane, and not thinking of ordinary mishaps, so a shout from above made me jump aside like a scalded cat. The contents of a chamber-pot just missed my head and hit the cobbles with a splash.

'Look who's below before you throw out your piss!' I shouted, and a woman's head in a mob cap appeared at a window, gave a mock expression of horror, grinned and disappeared. It was my neighbour Joel Andrews' maid, an over-pert though good-hearted wench. It is one of the disadvantages of living in Durn Lane which, being narrow, does not allow one to avoid rubbish and ordure being flung down from upper windows. In many ways, though, I was glad to live in a little back street, especially when at any time soldiers from one side or the other might come roistering through the town. The chances were that they would miss our Lane, and if they were breaking in and robbing would go to the wider streets and richer-looking houses.

I went on up the Lane and was almost at my shop when my next door neighbour, Tom Hartley the tailor, came rushing out of his door.

'Micah, have you heard? have you heard?'

Tom is always eager to be the first to tell of what's happening, and delights to pass it on to me.

'What now, Tom?'

'There's going to be a burning. They've caught a wizard or a he-witch or whatever you may call him. He's just been brought into town.'

'I know, I saw him.'

'Oh, so you know all about it.' Tom sounded disappointed. He's not a cruel man, but does enjoy it when his news is more grisly than usual.

'What makes you think he's going to be burned?' I asked.

'Well, 'tis plain, if he's a witch that's what'll happen to 'un.'

'But if he's not a witch he ought to be set free. So don't condemn the man, Tom, until you know the truth.'

I turned in at my shop and my heart lifted as I closed the door, feeling I was entering a haven safe from the hatreds and evils of the outside world. As I went through to the house behind I heard singing in the kitchen, where Hester our maid was preparing the meal, and more singing in the parlour, where my wife Agnes was sewing and watching over our son Mark, now a little over a year old. I kissed Agnes, who was big with our second child, due to be born in a few weeks, and knelt down to see what Mark was doing. He was playing with some odd bits of wood I had found for him, setting them up and knocking them down. 'Bang, bang,' he said. I thought rather sadly, these Civil Wars are even affecting babes.

I had been married two years ago this month, and counted myself very fortunate. I could not have married a more loving and lovely wife, though when I get into scrapes she sometimes has a sharp tongue. But that is because she fears for my safety. Her parents live outside the town walls in Fordington, which is like a part of the town spilling over towards the water-meadows, and they had become like second parents to me. My own father and mother died of the plague when I was small, and Aunt Alis who brought me up was also dead.

After we had eaten I had to attend to some things in my shop, then looked into the parlour before going out.

'I have to go to Wolfeton House,' I told Agnes. 'I may be away for an hour or two.'

'Is that to see the stable-boy?' she asked. I had told her how a few days before I had been called there to see the boy, young Robin, who had cut his hand.

'Yes, my dear, I have to change the dressing I put on the other day, and make sure the wound is healing properly. I'm rather afraid he will have been getting it dirty again if he's been working with the horses, though I told him to take special care of it.'

'I expect he has to do what the head groom tells him,' said Agnes. 'Anyway, dearest, be careful while you're outside the town.'

Wolfeton is only about a mile from Top o' Town, so I expected a safe and pleasant walk in the May sunshine, for though there were dangers further afield, with footpads and deserters likely to rob travellers, I did not anticipate any trouble so near to the town.

As I walked out of the town gate I thought how strange the times I lived in were, when, on such a lovely afternoon as this, in other parts of England armies were marching and fighting. Even in Dorset no doubt at this very moment less than thirty miles away at Lyme men—and women too—were wounding and killing each other. Lawrence Huatt had been sure that the King was still based at Oxford, being threatened by the Parliamentary commander, the Earl of Essex. Heaven alone knew where Prince Maurice's brother, Prince Rupert and his dreaded cavalry, might strike next, for although an army usually travels at walking pace horsemen may dash here and there and everywhere, bringing terror and death out of the blue.

Then there was the Royalist Lord Hopton somewhere in the south west, while Parliament's William Waller was also thought to be leading a powerful force, but where we did not know. We heard so many rumours of skirmishes, raids and battles, half of them no doubt untrue. I wondered idly how I would have done as a soldier.

Before Dorchester's surrender I had been a keen member of the militia, drilling and practising sword-play, and helping to patrol the walls. Since then we had not had many parades, though occasionally we stood guard at one or other of the town gates. As a boy I had been a proper little Puritan, a follower of our famous minister, the Reverend John White, and when the trouble between King and Parliament broke out I had no doubt which side I (and God) should support.

But after Mr White abandoned us, and those who had seemed so strong for our Cause faltered and gave in, I had lost my old certainty. I still called myself a Parliament man, a Roundhead even, but what I really hoped for was that Parliament and the King might come to some agreement together and end these dreadful wars.

Now, though, all seemed peaceful around Dorchester on this May afternoon. There were cows in the meadows down by the River Frome, and sheep dotted about on the higher ground by Poundbury Camp, the old British earth castle on the far side of the river. I began to hum a cheerful tune as I took a short cut through the meadows to the house.

Wolfeton is a compact old building, mostly of two stories arranged around a small courtyard. On its east front it has a very impressive gatehouse, which stands between round projecting towers with steep pointed roofs. The towers don't quite match, as the one on the left is wider than the other, and the gateway is not central between them, but off-set to one side. There are arrow-slits in the towers, but really they are just for show, as the walls are not very thick and the house could not sustain a siege.

It had its moment of fame long ago in Henry VII's time, when Archduke Philip of Austria and his Duchess Joanna were blown in to Weymouth in a storm. They were entertained at Wolfeton by the Trenchards, and a young man, John Russell, who could understand Spanish, was brought there to translate. That young man found favour at court, and became the first Earl of Bedford with a very great estate. The Trenchards still live at the old house.

I did not go through the gateway but turned right towards the stables, where I found Robin, the stable-boy, with a barrow and shovel cleaning out one of the stalls. He still had a bit of dirty bandage on his hand, but it looked as if it had bled some more since I last saw him.

'You silly boy,' I said. 'You must keep the cut clean and take care not to reopen the wound.'

'I'm sorry, Mr Judd,' he said.

'Don't be sorry for me,' I said, 'it's your hand you'll be in danger of losing if you don't look after it.'

''Tis hard to keep clean in the stables, Mr Judd,' he said. 'An' I've got to keep working or I'll lose my job. Mr Allen was angry enough wi' me for cutting meself.'

Mr Allen was the head groom.

'I'll have a word with him myself,' I said. I washed the boy's hand at the water-trough, and was fixing a clean bandage round it, when a lady rode into the yard. She was quite young, twenty-one or two I suppose, with gold, almost silver, hair and wearing a blue riding-dress. An under-groom ran across and held the horse as she dismounted.

'Who's that?' I asked Robin.

'Ah, 'tis Lady Alicia,' he said. 'She's a friend or cousin of Lady Trenchard's an' has come to stay for a bit.'

After exchanging a few words about her horse with the groom the lady walked across to us and asked what we were doing.

'Robin here cut his hand—a nasty wound,' I said. 'I bound it up last week, but he's opened the cut again and made it bleed. He shouldn't be doing this sort of work until it's healed.'

She asked me who I was, and when she heard I was an apothecary said she also might need my services.

'I'll tell Mr Allen to give Robin leave for a week or so. He can help in the kitchen perhaps, or do odd jobs around the garden. When you have finished here, Mr Judd, could you come and see me? I shall be sitting in the outer yard.'

She crossed the stable yard to speak to the head groom, who looked annoyed, but said, 'Yes, m'lady. All right, m'lady,' so I hoped he would do as she said.

When I had finished tying the bandage and giving Robin strict instructions to let his hand heal before he did more heavy work, I followed the lady into what she called the outer yard, which was a walled area in front of the gatehouse. She was sitting in the sun on a bench against a wall.

'Come and sit beside me, Mr Judd,' she said, 'and see if you can prescribe something for me.'

'What do you think is the matter?' I asked.

'If I knew, I could prescribe for myself. I am not sleeping well, I take no joy in food, I feel low and melancholy.'

'Have you any bodily sickness which might cause your feelings? Have you had headache, sore throat, any rheum or flux?'

'No, none of those. It is just that I feel a sort of deadness in my heart. It's as if some of the elixir of life has drained from me.'

'Did you enjoy your ride?'

'Oh yes,' she brightened, 'I had a wonderful gallop across

Charminster Down.'

'Did you feel ill as you rode?'

'No, with the wind in one's face and one's horse flying over the turf, how could one feel ill?'

'You might, if your sickness were of the body.'

'But when I come back here I do feel ill, listless, with no energy, no liveliness.'

'Did you begin to feel like this when you arrived here, or were you ill before?'

'At home I have felt melancholy at times. I live with my father in Hampshire, but he is often away. I have a brother, but he too is away—fighting for Parliament. If only I were a man I'd go and fight too. But what can a woman do? I wish I had been born a man!'

'Many people feel dull and heavy when they visit us in Dorset,' I said. 'There's something in the air here that makes them want to sleep. One would expect the nearness of the sea, with its bracing breezes, to make people more lively. But on the contrary, our air seems to encourage lethargy in those who are not used to it.'

'I know, I have noticed it before when I have come here, but the effect usually wears off after one has been here for a little. But my melancholy is due to more than the influence of the air, I think.'

'Lady,' I said, 'it seems to me that perhaps your sickness is of the spirit rather than the body. I have a powder of dried fumitory which may help to relieve it, and I will let you have some. But the best cure for melancholy is to be active and busy and to avoid sitting long in places where you may be tempted to mope. Doesn't being with Lady Trenchard help?'

'Yes, certainly, when she's here. But she and Sir Thomas are away at present. They are much occupied with the war, as no doubt you know.'

'I know he did much with Sir Walter Erle to prepare Lyme's defences. I wish he had been able to do more to stiffen Dorchester's resolve last year. But is he not getting rather old for taking an active part in fighting?' He certainly seemed an old man to me, for he was

(I believe) the wrong side of sixty at that time.

'Well, he has not wielded a sword for some while. But he has a lifetime of experience and much wisdom to impart. So he has much to do and much to offer in support of Parliament and true religion. He has gone to confer with the leading men in London, and also hopes to visit his old friend Robert.'

'Who is that, my lady?'

'Robert? Oh, the Earl of Essex. He and my father campaigned together in Germany.'

Lord Essex, as I have mentioned, was commander of the Parliamentary army, a very experienced soldier, much liked by his men, though I believe other commanders found him difficult to work with.

'So,' she went on, 'while they travel and are engaged on great affairs, I sit in the sun or ride or read or embroider. I only wish they had taken me with them.'

'Certainly travel and company can sometimes help to lift the spirits of those who are melancholic,' I said. 'New scenes, new people to meet, the bodily effort, all can have a good effect. But travel is not very safe in England at present.'

'I wouldn't mind the danger, and I am used to riding all over the place. I have a couple of trusty fellows to attend me, who are defence enough against common footpads. I could go off on my own with them, I suppose, but where? I would like to go and see Lord Essex myself. But there's no point. I have no part to play in the war.'

'You know Lord Essex then?'

'Yes, he dandled me on his knee when I was a girl. He and father used to meet sometimes and share memories of their old battles.'

'Well, my lady, maybe travel will soon be safer and you will be able to go. Meanwhile try a course of my powder, and keep as active as you can. Ride every day—try coming into Dorchester. You might find it beneficial to see if there is anything you could do in the neighbourhood, for there is much that needs doing. The poor, with all the shortages and rising prices, are in a bad way, and you might be able to help them, or do other works of charity—anything to avoid just sitting and allowing melancholy to settle upon you.'

'Thank you,' she said, 'I'm sure you are right. I shall come to your shop myself to collect the medicine, and will hope it may do me good. As for charity, I am not much fitted for it. I get too impatient when I see people waiting for others to help them, when I feel they could be helping themselves. I want to be involved in the war. I dream of riding across the country with dispatches, or doing something wild and heroic.' She laughed at herself, which seemed to me a good sign that her melancholy was not too deep-rooted and might be cured by the simple means I had suggested. 'I wish even as a woman I had a reason to ride somewhere,' she went on, 'but nobody would want to use a young woman like me, or entrust me with anything of importance!' She laughed again, a little bitterly.

'Who knows what may happen?' I said, standing up and smiling. 'In such times as these none of us know when we may be called upon to risk our very lives!'

Then, when I had explained to her how to find my shop, I took my leave.

I had spoken lightly, but all too soon my words would prove prophetic, as you shall hear.

Chapter 2 Prison

NEXT MORNING, as soon as I had a little time to spare, I walked down to the prison. Someone had written 'BURNE YE WITCH' in chalk on the wall, and underneath 'SATHAN IS HERE'.

I banged on the door without result, and only after I had given it another series of blows did the Keeper at last open it. He was a short stout fellow in a dirty leather jerkin, with thinning black hair and a very red nose with a wart on it.

'Yeah?' he said rudely.

'I've come to see one of your prisoners,' I said, 'Malachy Moore, who was brought in yesterday by the soldiers.'

'Him! You won't do no good visiting him! You won't get anything out o' him. No point in you're trying to see him.'

'Nevertheless I wish to do so.' I suspected the fellow was making things difficult in order to extract a larger tip from me.

'Well, sir, he's not said a word since they left him here, so I doubt you'll do any good. Furthermore, he might put the devil on you. He's a witch or wizard, no doubt about it, and I don't mind admitting I'm scared o' what he may put on me; an' the sooner they take an' burn him the better pleased I'll be.'

'Anyway, let me see him,' I said, and pressed a coin into his palm.

'Don't I know you?' he said, peering at me.

'Probably,' I answered. 'I'm Micah Judd the apothecary, with a shop in Durn Lane.'

'Oh-ah,' he said, 'I seen you about somewhere. Well, I s'pose you know what you're doing, but don't blame me if he puts the evil eye on you.'

He let me in and led me along a stone-flagged passage to a

heavy iron studded door. He slid back a little shutter and looked though a grating in the door and, having made sure that it was safe to do so, pulled back a couple of bolts and let me enter the prison hall. I heard the door shut behind me and the bolts being driven home as I looked at the scene.

It was a fairly large room, with a small barred window high up at the far end, bare stone walls, straw on the stone floor, a bucket in the corner and stone benches along each side. There were only two prisoners, though I suppose there may have been other rooms or cells elsewhere in the building.

A few months before quite a lot of men had been held here—not criminals, but Parliamentary supporters who had been imprisoned by the Royalists when they took over the town. This was after Dorchester had surrendered to Lord Carnarvon and Prince Maurice. The imprisonment and ill-treatment of some of my friends, and the arrogant behaviour of the Cavaliers, and the pillaging the Prince had allowed them to do, had sickened me.

So I had been pleased when the Roundheads hit back in December. Captain Francis Sydenham had come from Poole and taken over Dorchester for a few hours—and we didn't resist him either. He released the Parliament men from prison and carried off the chief Royalists of the town, including the Deputy Governor, William Churchill, and his assistant, Joseph Paty, and relieved another prominent Royalist, Robert Coker the goldsmith, of his gold and silver plate. Churchill and the others were soon allowed home after paying ransom money (which Sydenham called 'fines'), and had been warned not to ill-treat Parliamentary supporters in the town.

But I had been saddened that Dorchester, which had been such a peaceful and mostly tolerant place in the old days, was now so deeply divided. Some folk who had got on well enough with their neighbours a year or two ago now wouldn't even nod to those they thought of as enemies if they happened to pass in the street.

However, at present the prison was being used for its proper purpose, to hold those awaiting trial, either by the local justices at Quarter Sessions or at the twice yearly Assizes. In spite of the wars the justices and judges tried to keep the courts going, though of course there was some disruption. Normally the Quarter Sessions took place in a regular sequence at Blandford, Sherborne, Shaftesbury and Bridport. Sometimes, though, they were held at Dorchester, and this became more common during these disturbed times.

The smell which greeted me was almost overpowering at first—foul air, sweat, human excrement, unwashed clothes—but in my work one gets used to such things, and I walked across the straw-strewn flagstones, stepping carefully to avoid treading on anything nasty, to where Malachy was sitting. He and his companion gazed at me warily, no doubt wondering who I was and what I was doing there.

'Mr Moore,' I said, 'don't you remember me? You found that hidden hoard for me with your hazel rod.'

He gave me a hard stare. One of his eyes was still bruised and half closed, and he had blood and mud on his face, while his thin white hair was all in a tangle.

'I do mind ye,' he said at last in his high-pitched cracked voice, ''twere your friend's treasure that was hid in the wall.'

'That's right,' I said, 'I was grateful to you, and so was the owner of the money. I'm sorry to see you here like this.'

'They git me at last—I knew they would. The Church an' the Law, they git a man in the end, come what may.'

'Look out, mister,' said the other prisoner. 'He's a witch, he is. He's going to be burned. He'll put the evil eye on you if you don't watch out.'

'Who are you, friend?' I asked.

'Robert Still, that's me. I'm a respectable thief, I am. They shouldn't put me in with muck like him. I complained to the Keeper, but he don't listen. I shall tell the justices though. It ain't right.'

I turned back to Malachy.

'How did you get in this trouble?' I asked.

'They were out to git me,' he said.

'Who? Who set that mob on you?'

'Why are you axing all this, zur? Are you a lawyer?'

'No, no. As I told you when I met you before, I'm an apothecary. And because you helped me then I'd like to help you now, if I can. For example, I could find you a lawyer if you like.'

'I don't want no lawyers,' he said, striking his right fist against his left palm with surprising force. 'I don't hold wi' lawyers, blood-suckers.'

'But if you don't put up some sort of defence you'll be condemned.'

'Yeah,' said the other prisoner derisively, 'he'll burn, that he will!'

''Tis true,' said Malachy, shrinking into himself on the bench, 'they'll kill me right enough.'

'But they must have something against you,' I protested. 'It's not enough just to say a man's a witch or wizard. There must be some proof.'

'They say I killed Mr Godwin.'

'And did you?'

His face took on a wary crafty look.

'I wouldn' say if I had, now, would I?' he said.

'Well, what made them think you had?'

'He died, didn' 'un?'

'But what connection did you have with him?' I was feeling angry and frustrated at having to drag the information from him in such small portions.

'He said he owned the land my cottage is on. That's what he said, though 'twere a lie an' I didn' believe 'un.'

'So...?'

'He were trying to get me out. He's a lawyer, see.'

'So what did you do?'

'I cussed him.'

'Well, we all swear at other people sometimes.'

'You don't understand, zur. I cussed him an' he died.'

'But surely your curse can't have killed him? What did he die of?'

'He died after I cussed 'un. I said, "Your guts'll rot, cuss you! The fire'll burn you within, cuss you. May you fall senseless and not arise, cuss you. Cuss you to hell!" That's what I told 'un.'

'What happened?'

'It all happened, just as I said.'

'And did other people hear you say this curse?'

'Aye, there were one or two who did, an' when he died they called it to mind and stirred up their fellows. They came buzzin' about me like bees, a-shoutin' an' a-hollerin', and dragged me out, and cried out for my blood, an' pulled me this way an' that, an' carried me to the mill-pond an' would ha' thrown me in if they so'jers hadn' come.'

I looked at him in silence for a moment. For all I knew he might indeed be in league with the devil, and I shuddered inwardly at the thought. I remembered a sermon of Mr White's in which he had terrified us by describing the fate of those who have dealings with Satan. But on the other hand Malachy might merely be a harmless old person, a bit odd, a bit crusty, with some special gifts (like that with the hazel rod), but no great evil. He looked so helpless, so beaten down, and yet he had a kindly face. Surely an evil wizard ought to look more devilish? And why, if he had supernatural powers, did he seem so powerless?

'You're not really an evil person, in league with Satan?' I said doubtfully. 'You didn't really mean this Mr Godwin to die like that?'

'I did want him to lay off me, dead or living. But you're wrong about me, zur, for I be a very evil person, zur. Passon told me so, an' cast me out o' the church, not to be buried in holy ground, not to go to heaven.'

'Nonsense,' I said, 'you're being a very silly old man!'

I said this without thinking, for I was feeling impatient with his meek acceptance of the role people seemed to have given him. Also I suppose I wanted strongly to deny that he might be devil-possessed because, I must admit, I was a little afraid, for if he really was a witch it would be dangerous for all who had dealings with him, including me. Yet my reason told me that he was just a poor confused old man. But he seemed intent not to help himself, but rather to stir up my fears.

'You came to see me at hwome, zur. You saw the powers at work,' he said. 'You saw the spirits working through my hazel wand. Alas, zur, 'tis not a power I would seek, for it's brought me to ruin, but I cannot avoid it. My words struck home to 'un an' he died.'

'I cannot help you if you persist in saying that,' I said. 'It's probably against the law to curse as you did, quite apart from any witchcraft. You've already said too much.'

'I can testify to what he's said,' Robert Still interposed. 'He can't go back on it now. He's got to be burned.'

'You be quiet,' I said. 'You had better prepare you own defence, rather than interfere with this man. They hang thieves more often than they burn witches.'

He drew back muttering angrily, and I turned to Malachy.

'Is there nothing I can do for you?' I asked.

'There is, zur, if you would be zo kind. It's my puss, my dear old Simmany. If you would be passin' by Upwey an' could look in at my cottage, an' take care of 'un if he be there. I do fear he may be hurt or starven.'

'I'll do that,' I promised, 'I will make the journey there tomorrow. But is there nothing I can do for you here?'

'Thank ye, zur, if you do see to Simmany there's nothin' more I do need.' He shrank back again on the bench and seemed to hunch up small and vulnerable. I walked over to Robert Still.

'Listen here,' I said sternly, 'you will leave Mr Moore alone, and not torment him in any way. If I hear that you have hurt or harmed him by word or deed I will personally make sure you are hanged. Do you understand?'

He looked daggers at me, but muttered, 'Yes, sir.'

I thumped on the door and called for the Keeper, who came in his unhurried fashion to let me out. As I stepped with relief into the free open air and took a deep breath I began to have second thoughts. Was I being utterly foolish to get myself involved with Malachy, particularly when he seemed so determined not to be helped? Yet in my heart I knew I could not stand aside and watch this feeble old man being hounded to his death. I had benefited from his skill with the hazel twig and had come to the conclusion that it was a God-given gift and not evil. So why should I now fear that he might be devilish? I felt, too, that behind the death of Mr Godwin there must be more than a simple curse. Someone else might have murdered him, and I wanted to find out more.

But nevertheless I was wary. The devil comes in many disguises, and goes about seeking to destroy souls, and might have taken possession of this poor old man for all I knew. And his cat, which I had seen and even touched when I had first met him, might be simply a cat, but (as the carter had tried to say) it could be an incubus or evil familiar spirit. If it were, I would be putting my soul in grave danger by caring for it. But I comforted myself with the thought that our Lord is more powerful than any evil spirit, and would (I believed) protect me.

As I walked back up the High Street I had a vivid reminder of how bitterly divided Dorchester had become as a result of the Civil War and our surrender to the Royalists. Not only the country was divided, but also the county and even single families, father against son, or brother against brother. A little crowd was standing in Cornhill at the junction with South Street, and as I drew near I could hear voices raised in anger.

'You filthy son of Belial, thou hast betrayed the Lord and dragged His Name in the dust.'

'Call not me a betrayer, thou traitor to thy King!'

I pushed past some bystanders and saw two respectable Dorchester citizens standing a little apart with clenched fists and red faces. Edward Barton the mercer and John Haggard the clothier.

'I am no traitor,' shouted Barton, 'the Lord knows I would die for the King if he would free himself from his popish advisers and hold a free Parliament. But thou, thou Romish dog, wouldst have us all in chains.'

'I am no Roman, and that thou knowest. I am a Church of England man, and want none of your Covenants and Conventicles,' Haggard retorted. 'Get thee back to hell, where thou belongest!'

'Nay, I could not stand the stink of thee there. Thou'lt have to go there on thine own.'

It was so childish that I would have laughed if it wasn't also so unhappy. But it would have got worse, for Haggard stepped forward as if he would have struck Barton had not two of the bystanders interposed.

'Come, John,' said one, 'don't mind him. He will keep on.'

'Aye,' said Haggard, 'the devil never rests.'

At that Barton also had to be restrained and was persuaded by his friends to leave, but shouted over his shoulder as he went, 'Thou hast the mark of Satan, and he has a place for thee in hell!'

As I walked on I was joined by my neighbour, Joel Andrews the tanner (the one whose maid had nearly doused me with her chamber-pot), who had evidently seen and heard it all.

'That was a lively spat,' he said. 'Those two know how to ballywrag each other!'

'What was it all that about?'

'I don't rightly know. They met here at the corner and just started abusing each other.'

'Tempers have been short of late,' I said, 'ever since the Cavaliers came into the town.'

'That's a sure thing,' he agreed. 'There'll be no peace here till one or the other party gets the upper hand.'

But it seemed to me that even if neither King or Parliament beat the other quickly, and the war went on, the townsfolk of Dorchester would have to go on dwelling together, and would have to learn to live and let live.

A little later I went to see Nathan Whittle, the glover, whose money it was that Malachy had found with his hazel rod. It had been all of Nathan's savings, including his daughter's dowry, which had been stolen and hidden by a thieving soldier. Nathan had been exceedingly grateful to get it back, and I hoped he would help in Malachy's defence.

He greeted me warmly:

'Good morning, Micah, a lovely day. You are well I trust?'

'Thank you, yes. But have you a moment, Mr Whittle? There's something I want to consult you about.'

'Of course, of course, I'm always ready to serve you.'

I sat down on a stool and asked after his daughter.

'Elizabeth is well. You were right—that young man she's married is proving a good husband, and doing well in his shop they tell me. And now Elizabeth is expecting, as is your Agnes, I believe?'

I said how pleased I was for Elizabeth, and that Agnes was going on well as far as I knew, and then he asked:

'What do you want to consult me about? I'll always be pleased to help in any way I can.'

'Do you remember when I brought your money back, how I told you about the Wise Man of Upwey, who found where it had been hidden? Well, now he's in trouble and needs our help.'

'I'm sorry to hear that. What sort of trouble?'

'He's in the town gaol. He was brought in yesterday from Upwey. Some soldiers out on patrol found the village people about to drown him in the mill-pond, saying he was a wizard or a witch. Apparently a man died, and they're accusing Malachy of causing the death by witchcraft.'

'Oh dear, oh dear, I heard about a he-witch being brought into custody,' he said, getting quite agitated, 'but I had no idea that it was that man. After you brought my money back, and told me it had been found with a divining rod, I was worried that the devil might have had a hand in it. But as it seemed to have brought good to me I hoped the Lord would overlook any fault in the way it was found. But remember what Saint Peter saith, the devil "walketh about as a roaring lion, seeking whom he may devour", always trying to tempt us to perdition. It could endanger our immortal souls if we were to become involved with this man.'

'But Malachy seems to me a good old man. He's a bit odd, as old people often become when they live alone. But he doesn't seem to me to be possessed by the Evil One. There's no smell of brimstone about him.'

'Oh dear, oh dear,' Whittle said again, 'I don't think I want anything to do with the devil.'

'But you're not listening to me, Nathan. I'm telling you that as far as I can see Malachy has not anything to do with the devil. He may have dabbled in forbidden things, but we have no knowledge of that. We know he has skill with the hazel rod, but I have heard of others with that gift, and they were not witches. It may be a natural gift that the Lord bestows on some, as He does the gift of music or painting or even'—I added with a smile—'making gloves.'

'I don't like it, Micah. I've always kept clear of the devil, as far as a Christian may. Really, I don't want to be involved.'

'But would you allow him to die, wrongfully accused? The thing they're accusing him of—killing a man by cursing—I suppose is possible, but I won't believe in it until I see proper proof.'

'Oh my dear God!' Whittle exclaimed, 'is that what they accuse him of? For love of the Lord, keep away from him, Micah, lest he curse you too.'

'Do be calm, Nathan. I'm going to make some enquiries about the man he's supposed to have killed. I very much doubt if

Malachy's curses are so powerful. I smell something odd about all this, and (as you know) I have a nose for such things, and I mean to find out the truth. If Malachy has really sold himself to the devil he has made a very poor bargain, for he's in a miserable state at present. However, if I do find he's been dabbling in witchcraft I'll wash my hands of him. But if I find he merely let fly with some curses, perhaps with good reason, and the man happened to die from other causes, even if Malachy himself believes that his curses made it happen, I don't think—after all he did for us—that we ought to let him burn.'

'If he cursed the man, and the man died, this Malachy fellow deserves to die anyway.'

'Oh come, Nathan, haven't you ever cursed someone when you were angry? What about that sergeant who stole your money? I'll wager you cursed him—and he died, didn't he? Does that make you a witch?'

'Well,' he mumbled, 'what do you want me to do?'

'Be on hand to speak up for him if he comes to trial. Be willing, if necessary, to stand surety for him.'

'Oh dear, oh dear, I don't like being mixed up in this sort of thing. People have such strong feelings about anything to do with the devil—they might start to think I had dealings with the Evil One myself.'

'But you want to see justice done, and it won't be unless we stand up for this old man. So will you help?'

'I'll—oh, very well if you insist, I'll help as far as I can,' he gave his reluctant promise. With that I had to be content, though I feared that such half-hearted support would do Malachy little good if he came to trial.

I returned home and was soon busy in the shop, seeing several customers and preparing syrups and pills. In the afternoon a lady entered—Lady Alicia from Wolfeton.

Her coming seemed to bring a ray of light into my shop.

Perhaps it was a glint of sunlight on her hair and the brightness of her blue cloak. But there was also a sparkle in her eyes and a smile on her lips.

'See,' she said, 'I have come myself for the medicine, and feel better for the ride, though last night after I saw you, I felt low again.'

'I have your medicine ready, my lady,' I said. 'Take a spoonful night and morning in water, and keep doing things—riding, walking, meeting people—rather than sitting by yourself and allowing the melancholy to settle upon you.'

'I shall try,' she said, 'but it is wearisome longing to do something important in the world, yet feeling one is useless.'

'Who knows? You may suddenly be called upon to do some great work, like Lady Bankes defending Corfe.'

It was not perhaps the best example to give to an ardent supporter of Parliament, for Lady Bankes had held Corfe Castle for the King against all assaults the previous year, and the Roundheads had abandoned the siege in confusion. However, Lady Alicia smiled and said, 'I hope you're right, though even if I was in command at Wolfeton I do not think it could withstand an enemy for long, for it is no castle. However, you incline to Parliament I'm told, so if you think of anything I could do, let me know.'

She said it lightly, paid me and left with her medicine, but I felt she would be delighted if I could tell her of a dragon to slay or some such heroic deed to be done.

A little later a girl, or rather a young woman, came in and waited until another customer had left. She was wearing a plain linen dress but with an expensive-looking lace collar and a dark green bonnet which showed off her fair hair to perfection. I guessed she was the daughter of one of the better off merchants or shop-keepers of the town.

When we were alone she came near and said in a low voice:

'Sir, do you have any potion that can alter people's opinions?'

I laughed and said, 'Medicines affect the body. You need

arguments to change the mind.'

'But you have love philtres, don't you?'

'Not I. You might find one in the market, sold by a mountebank or quacking doctor, but whether it would have any effect I doubt. But I doubt also,' I added smiling, 'that a young lady like you would need it. However, I do have medicines which can help to calm the mind or lift the spirits or help one sleep, if any of those would be of use.'

She looked rather downcast.

'It's not a love potion I want,' she said. 'I have his love, all of it, I know. But it's his parents and mine I need to change. Have you nothing that I could put in their food or drink which would make them friends?'

'Alas no,' I said, 'but there may be other means of achieving what you want. People can and do change, if one can but find the way to their hearts.'

'I have tried, and so has Matthew. But father is set against him, and his father is set against me.'

'And you are...?'

'Rachel Haggard. My father is Mr John Haggard the clothier. He's come out more strongly for the King of late, and calls all of a different mind traitors and outlaws.'

'Oh yes,' I said, 'I heard him myself this morning name-calling with Mr Barton in the open street.'

'Oh dear—I did so hope they wouldn't meet until they are less heated. Mr Barton is Matthew's father, you see. He's a very strict Puritan, and will no more allow his son to marry a Royalist's daughter than my father would let me be joined to a Roundhead. Matthew says his father thinks all Royalists support the Pope and want to change religion. But it's not true. Father is as good a Protestant as Mr Barton. It's just that he believes in the Church of England and bishops and organs and such things, while Mr Barton wants nothing but preachers in black gowns.'

'You and your Matthew are in a sad case then,' I said, 'for men's religious beliefs are harder to reconcile even than their politics. But even so they may be brought to accept one another as fellow Christians, I hope. Many men and women have married across the gulf that divides us. Why, most of the gentry have relations on both sides, and intermarry freely in spite of the wars.'

'I know,' she said, 'but father regards even being civil to those he calls "the enemy" as letting down the King. He would be furious if he knew I was seeing Matthew, and Mr Barton would be just as angry if he knew Matthew was seeing me.'

'Be patient, if you can,' I said. 'Time can work wonders. Just as we can't know whether King or Parliament will be winning in three months time, so you can't know how changed your situation may be by then. Your parents may change, circumstances will certainly change. Remember the old Dorsetshire saying, "Things do come around"—and they often do, you know.'

'It would be much easier if I could put some medicine in father's food or drink to change him.'

'That's true,' I agreed, 'but unfortunately I know of no such thing, so I can only say again, "Be patient", and all may yet be well.'

It struck me that I was telling many people to be patient and they would see a way out of their troubles—easy advice to give, and yet I was sure it was right. Particularly in war-time many things might quickly alter.

She gave me a thoughtful look, then turned to leave, saying over her shoulder, 'Why do people have to hate and fight each other? If it weren't for Matthew I think I would wish I were dead!'

Chapter 3 On the trail of evil

I WENT OUT to the back-yard early next morning to saddle my horse—the precious horse that I had been enabled to afford because of the rewards Nathan Whittle and others had given me for recovering their treasures. Leaving Agnes to mind the shop, I was soon trotting out of South Gate and along the old Roman road, chalky white, with gravel in the worst pot-holes, past the turnings to Herringston and Monkton, and slowing to a walk as we began to climb the long hill to the ridge which separates Dorchester from the coast. An even more ancient road, the Ridgeway, along which long-dead traders and warriors tramped east or west, crosses to the left and right just before the summit. Then as I went over the ridge I saw the land spread out below me as far as the coast, with beyond it the sea grey and (seen from this distance) apparently calm, and the bulk of Portland rearing up dark and menacing in the background.

Portland with its castle, Weymouth and its twin town Melcombe, and Sandsfoot Castle near Weymouth, were at this time all in the hands of the Royalists, having been captured (as I have described in my account of the Three Treasures) by Prince Maurice during his triumphant campaign the previous August. Portlanders had welcomed the Cavaliers, because the Roundhead Governor, Captain Arthur, had been hated for his depredations and for driving out their beloved Rector, Doctor Humphrey Henchman. From my point of view Captain Arthur had been captured in the nick of time, because he had had me in his power and was likely to have hanged me as a spy. But Weymouth and Melcombe were, like Dorchester, divided in opinions. I wondered whether they, having more soldiers quartered among them than we did, were getting more tired of their conquerors.

I rode down the steep hill and turned right through the hamlet of

Elwell. The Manor House and another mansion were on my left as I turned up beside the little river, the Wey, and drew near to Upwey. I passed the church and soon after that reached Malachy's cottage, more decrepit than I remembered from my previous visit. The thatch was more ragged, a window shutter had been wrenched half off its hinges, and the door was swinging open.

I dismounted and hitched my horse's reins to a post, and stood for a moment taking in the scene. A broken crock lay in the doorway, and when I looked inside the cottage it seemed that everything had been smashed. The broken remains of Malachy's few bits of furniture, table, stool and bed, lay splintered on the floor with more pieces of smashed pottery. A dark lump stuck all over with pins and nails had been placed on the window-sill, and I guessed that it was a pig's heart, no doubt put there by one of the villagers to ward off the powers of evil.

In the fireplace was a black thing, part covered with a piece of rag. I moved the rag and saw that it was all that was left of Simmany, Malachy's cat. Its head had been smashed with something hard, probably the heavy stick or club that also lay amongst the ashes. The senseless violence done to the poor cat and to everything in the cottage saddened me.

I went outside and along beside the cottage to the little garden sloping steeply up the hill behind. It had been trampled by many rough boots and the few plants pulled up or trodden down. A spade was leaning against the back wall of the cottage. I balanced it on my hand while I looked at the scene, then impulsively dug a hole in a corner of the garden. Then I fetched Simmany's body, pushing the spade under it to raise it from among the ashes. It had started to stink, and I coughed and took a deep breath of fresh air as I carried it out of the door and around to the garden. There I placed the body in the hole, shovelled in the soil and put a large stone on top. I felt relieved when I had finished, and oddly pleased with what I had done, for Malachy would surely have been very hurt if his beloved cat had been left to rot in the wreckage.

As I came round to the front again I found a man was standing on the other side of the road looking at me. It was the carter who had been forced to bring Malachy to Dorchester.

'What are you doing there?' he demanded roughly. 'You be in danger o' meeting the devil there!'

'Why is that?' I asked, for it was clear that he did not recognise me.

'Don't ye know? That's where the he-witch did live. He's gone to Dorchester to be burned, but his devils may be still lurking hereabouts.'

'What devils are those?'

'All sorts o' devils. There was one in the shape of a black cat, a very terrible one that, an' others you could only see out o' the corner of your eye, lurkin' in the corners or up the chimney.'

'Did you see them?'

'Oh 'ees, some o' them. The one like a cat, now, he were enough to make your hair stand on end, terrifying he were. I tell you, sir, we sleep easier in our beds now that ol' witch has gone.'

'And his cottage—what's going to be done with this place? Who does it belong to now?'

'Ah, that's not certain. Some said it belonged to the witch himself, passed down from his granfer, I b'lieve. But the man he murdered claimed it, so I expect Sir James Freke will take it now, and who's to stop him?'

'What would the gentleman want a tumble-down little place like this for?'

'Oh, he owns the cottages on both sides, an' he'll pull 'em all down and build one bigger house here. Old Malachy has long been in his way, wouldn't move out although Sir James offered him a place at t'other end o' village. I reckon his devils didn't want him to move, an' I wouldn't be surprised if they do work to bring bad luck to Sir James too.'

He made a furtive sign to avert the evil, and spat to his left.

'But why do you say this man you call a witch murdered

someone?' I asked.

'Because that's indeed what he did with his evil arts. 'Twere this gentleman I mentioned, come from Melcombe, used to visit here quite often, Sir James being his cousin, you see.'

'What happened?'

'He come to visit, an' happened to come this end o' the village, an' had words with old Malachy—that's the witch. I wasn't by here myself to hear what was said, but I believe Mr Godwin, that's the gentleman from Melcombe, told Malachy he'd have to get out. There was some lawyers' decision about the land, or summat like that. Anyway, Malachy started to cuss and call up his devils, an' Mr Godwin fell down dead in the street.'

'What happened then?'

'People heard summat going on, an', as I said, we've long been afeard o' Malachy an' his devils. Someone shouted that we must get rid of the witch, and they dragged him down to the mill-pond to see if he'd float—witches do, you know, you can't keep 'em under—but a bunch o' so'jers came by an' stopped 'em.'

'Go on,' I said.

'Them so'jers made me carry 'un all the way to Dorchester in me cart, for they said he must have a proper trial. 'Tweren't a kindness really, for now he'll hang or burn instead o' drowning. But there, one can't argue wi' so'jers. They never paid me a penny for carting 'un though.'

'Who broke up the cottage?'

'Everybody. When the so'jers made 'em give him up, folks came back here, I believe. I wasn't here myself, for as I told you they made me carry him to Dorchester. But everyone came and broke the place up to destroy the power o' the devil. He can't work through broken things, they say. But I wouldn't go in there, if I were you, sir, for the devils may still be a-lurking.'

I thanked him for his advice, and walked my horse back a short way to the churchyard wall. There was no more to be discovered at the cottage, but the carter had given me food for thought. All that mess and destruction and smell of death had made me feel the presence of something sinister, and now the carter's words had stirred in me the fears that I had tried to quench, the thought that Malachy might really have been in league with evil powers. With an effort I told myself, 'that carter is an ignorant fellow, whose attitude is the all too common one of such fools'. For why (I argued with myself) should I jump to the conclusion that because a poor old person lives alone with a cat he or she must be a witch?

Also what they had done to Malachy's cottage and to Simmany disgusted me. This was the real evil, I told myself, when neighbours turn into wild beasts and persecute a harmless old man. How is it, I wondered, that Christian people are so afraid of the devil, when they ought to believe that our Lord has overcome the power of Satan?

And why were they so afraid of such a poor old man? The devil's servants (if witches really are such) so often seem feeble, and are so easily captured or killed, like poor old Malachy and his cat Simmany. If the devil is really so powerful why doesn't he protect his servants better?

I suppose a minister would say that the devil doesn't intend to keep his servants happy or safe. All he wants is for them to be damned, and if they suffer misery or pain on the way, so much the better. The devil may be powerful, but it still seems illogical to me if sober Christian men fear old women or cats or toads!

Nevertheless, having left my horse tethered at the churchyard gate where he could nibble some grass, on entering the church I said a prayer for protection from the Evil One, and felt better. Then I sat on a bench while I thought what to do next.

There was something odd about this affair, I was sure of it, but didn't know what. What part did Sir James Freke play in it all? Could he have made use of his cousin's death to get Malachy out of his way? He could not have arranged for Mr Godwin to die in order for Malachy to be accused of witchcraft, of course. But he might have taken advantage of what had happened. Then what was his feeling for his cousin? Were they friends, or enemies? It seemed they were friends, in that Godwin apparently visited quite often. Also, which of them had been trying to get Malachy out of his cottage? Or were the cousins working together to get him out? I must find out more about Mr Godwin and exactly how he died.

My glance wandered round the church, and I noticed to the right of the door a text had been newly painted on the whitewashed wall—some verses from the Book of Proverbs: *My son, fear thou the LORD and the king, and meddle not with them that are given to change. For their calamity shall rise suddenly, and who knoweth the ruin of them both?*

Well, these cousins had been meddling, and one had come to ruin; but calamity had also come to old Malachy. Of course the verses had probably been put there by a Royalist vicar or churchwarden to teach the villagers to submit to their betters and their king, which might imply that there were some rebellious elements among them.

I heard footsteps and the door creaked open. A clergyman entered, dressed soberly in black and holding his hat in his hand. He had a thin grey face, thinning grey hair and pale thin lips. Perhaps the text had been his choice. He gave me a hard stare, but greeted me civilly enough:

'Good day to you sir. I saw your horse at the gate. You are a stranger in these parts, I think?'

'Yes,' I said, 'I am Micah Judd, apothecary of Dorchester.'

'You are far from home, sir. What brings you here? Are you here to practise your profession? Can I perhaps be of assistance to you?'

'Indeed you may be,' I said, 'for I am an acquaintance of one of your flock who is in trouble, Malachy Moore from the cottage yonder.'

The parson's response was surprisingly violent.

'He is none of my flock! He is of his father the devil, and must suffer the just punishment for his sins in this world and eternal damnation in the next!'

'But what has he done?'

'What has he not done! He has long refused my admonitions. A blasphemer, sir, a son of Belial, a limb of Satan! It is well that he lies in gaol in Dorchester, and will soon be condemned, for hell's mouth is already gaping wide to receive him, and this world will be a better place when he is gone!'

'That is a terrible condemnation, sir. How can he deserve it?'

'He is the mouthpiece of the devil. He has long been a practiser of evil arts, but now he has gone further: he has cursed a man and killed him.'

'But do you really think he could kill a man by cursing?'

'By cursing and by his devilish arts, not a doubt about it, sir. Mr George Godwin, the man he killed, was a godly man, though not quite of my persuasion, and his cousin here, Sir James Freke, is a great supporter of the King and the Church.'

'What exactly happened to Mr Godwin?'

'He was riding back along the road, I understand, with Moore's curses still ringing in his ears, when suddenly they took effect. He was seized with sickness, managed to dismount and stagger to a cottage, and tried to rid himself of the devil by violent vomitings. But soon he fell into a paralytic fit, fainted away and died.'

'But why do you suspect Malachy Moore of causing his death? After all, many men curse others when they're angry.'

'It was plain, made all too plain by what followed. He cursed Mr Godwin, and Mr Godwin fell dead. Malachy Moore has put himself beyond redemption, he has sold himself to Satan. A terrible thing it is when a man gives himself over to the devil. For a short while the Evil One gives him power in exchange for an eternity of torment.'

I began to feel there was little hope for Malachy if even an educated parson indulged in this sort of logic. However, there seemed little benefit to be got from further discussion, so I asked the vicar which cottage Mr Godwin had gone to when he fell ill.

'Why do you want to know?' he asked suspiciously.

'As I told you, I am an apothecary, and so am interested in unusual symptoms of illness. I want to see how the work of the devil differs from plain poisoning.'

My irony was lost upon him, but he accepted my explanation and told me how to find the cottage.

Following his directions, I rode further down the village street till I found it, dismounted and knocked on the door. A plump woman in a dirty bonnet and apron looked out.

'I am an apothecary, Micah Judd of Dorchester,' I said, 'and I—'

'We want nothing with apothecaries,' she broke in.

'But as such I am interested in sudden deaths, and I believe it was here that Mr Godwin died.' I gave her a small coin, and her attitude changed.

'Indeed yes, sir. A terrible thing it was, sir. It made me quite faint an' my heart went bumpity-bump. Gave me a turn, it did, and I hope I never have such another. I mean, it's not a thing you want every day, a gentleman knocking on the door and falling dead at your feet, as it were. But come in, sir, and I'll show you the very spot.'

I hitched the horse to a hurdle by the door, and ducked low to enter the cottage. It had a plain floor of beaten earth, a big fireplace, a table, some stools and a chair.

''Twere there, sir,' she said, pointing at the chair . 'He came to the door an' said, "Can I come in an' sit for a moment. I feel most strange". Those were his very words, "I feel most strange". But if he was bewitched he would feel strange, wouldn't he, sir? Then he cried out, "The devil!", and was sick, most horribly sick. I got a basin for him, but it was too late—he sicked on the floor an' on his britches. Then he groaned a bit an' said, "Devil take it". You see, sir, how he kept harping on the devil? Then he cried out, "I can't move, I can't move", an' slid off the chair onto the floor an' lay there in a faint.'

'What happened then?'

'I called out to the neighbours. Some of 'em were already coming to help, an' one of 'em ran to fetch Sir James—the gentleman's cousin, you know—but before he could get here the poor gentleman was already dead. Then someone said how Malachy Moore had been cursing him. "That wicked old man," says Sir James, "he's killed him with his evil arts". An' then Tom Wayte shouted, "Let's go get him!" an' they ran up the street shouting that they would kill the witch, an' a'most everyone ran out to join them.'

'What did Sir James do?'

'He watched the people running up the street, an' then he said in a straining sort of way, as if he was nearly overcome, "I'll send to take this gentleman's body away. He comes from Melcombe an' will have to go there for burial." An' then he left.'

'Didn't he stop to see what they were doing to old Malachy?'

'Oh no, sir. I don't suppose he wanted to interfere, upset as he was at his cousin's death.'

'Upset, was he?'

'Oh yes, sir, so upset he could hardly speak.'

'So was Mr Godwin's body taken to Melcombe?'

'I suppose so, sir. Sir James's man came later on wi' a waggon an' took it away. 'Twere only an hour or two later that he came, soon after the so'jers had gone off wi' Malachy.'

There seemed little more that the woman could tell me, for she merely repeated how horrible and devilish the death of Mr Godwin had been, 'on that very chair, sir, I've hardly liked to sit on it since!'

'Where could I find the man who took the body away?' I asked.

'He might be up at Sir James' stables, beside the big house down the road there.' She came to the window and pointed, then added, 'But look, sir, if you want to speak to him you're in luck, for there's the very man going past now.'

I hurried out of the door and saw a stocky young fellow with short bristly brown hair looking at my horse in an admiring way, so I went over to him.

'Do you like the look of him?' I asked.

'Yes, sir,' he said. 'Is he fast?'

'Fast enough. He's a good stayer, which is even better. You

look as if you know something of horses.'

'Yes,' he said, 'I'm Sir James Freke's groom.'

'Ah,' said I, 'then you will be the man who took Mr Godwin home—or rather his body?'

'Yes, an' a doleful load it were. I had to drown myself in ale afterwards to take away the flavour o' it.'

'Has he been buried yet, do you know?'

'He's being buried today, sir, I believe. 'Tis all in a hurry, with him not three days dead. But Sir James wanted his black hoss saddled this morning, an' has gone off in his best cloak, an' I did hear say they were burying the gentleman at Radipole this very day.'

'Ought not the coroner to sit and enquire?' I wondered. 'It was such a sudden death.'

'I don't know about that, sir. Maybe he sat at Melcombe. But I don't suppose Sir James would wait for a coroner. An impatient man is our Sir James, sir; he won't brook anyone getting in his way.'

'Had Mr Godwin been to see Sir James the day he died, do you know?'

'Yes, sir, I believe they dined together, and I saw Mr Godwin ride off. He must ha' died very soon after.'

'Did he seem ill when you saw him?'

'I didn't notice particularly. He seemed in a hurry, I thought.'

I decided to ride on the couple of miles or so to Radipole to see if there was anything further to be learned, but before I did so I asked the groom what the state of things was in Melcombe, and whether there were soldiers about; for I did not want to meet any who might steal my horse or do me violence.

'Oh, 'tis all quiet there now, I think you'll find,' he said. 'The so'jers are mainly t'other side o' the river, and don't seem to interfere with folks much at present. Not like when they first came. They were swarming all over the place then, like bees, an' bees with stings! But if you're going that way I'd say you'll be all right in Melcombe, but I'd keep away from Weymouth, if I were you, sir.'

I thanked him and rode off. Melcombe and Weymouth are officially one town now, but they've always been divided by the river and only joined by a drawbridge, and the people of the two places still keep up much of their old rivalry, even enmity.

I came out onto the main Roman road again, and turned right towards Melcombe. I was still in two minds about what I had heard. Certainly Malachy had strange gifts, and most of the people I had talked to about him were utterly convinced that he had been in touch with the devil. But his gifts had done him no good, and in prison he seemed so helpless. Surely an evil wizard ought to have greater powers! Mr Godwin had undoubtedly died after Malachy had cursed him, but was there any connection between the curse and his death? The manner of his death sounded to me much more like the result of poison, perhaps something eaten by chance, or maybe deliberately given. Aconite poisoning, for example, could have had the effects which had been described to me, though how it could have been administered puzzled me. Also I knew of no one who had a motive for killing him, apart that is from Malachy, and he had had no chance to tamper with Godwin's food. I wondered what Sir James had given him to eat.

But then his death might have been due to illness or a fit or some other natural cause. Certainly the coroner ought to have made an enquiry. That set me thinking more about Sir James. Why (if the groom was right) would he not want the coroner involved? Could he have a motive for doing away with his cousin? Mr Godwin had visited him that day, and the meal would have provided the opportunity to poison him. But would the poison have taken so long to act? Could Godwin have ridden up the village and had a meeting with Malachy before feeling its effects? And was it significant that Sir James had apparently encouraged the villagers to blame the death on old Malachy? There were so many questions which needed answers.

I turned down the lane towards Radipole church, which is a small old building on the brow of the hill which slopes down towards the river, where marshy land is mostly covered with water at high tide. Strangely enough this little church, which only has a small hamlet around it, is the mother-church of Melcombe a mile or two to the south. They have a fairly new church in the town, but often still come out to Radipole for funerals.

As I drew near I could see some horses tethered near the gate, and a cart draped in black which had evidently been used as a hearse. People were beginning to come away from the churchyard, and it was clear that a funeral was just over. I hoped it had been Mr Godwin's, and that I might learn something more from some of the mourners. So I dismounted and waited for them to come out, meanwhile wondering how I could get into conversation with someone who might know more of what had caused the death.

A man in a rich cloak seemed to be the chief mourner, a tall man with bushy black eyebrows and a little pointed beard and a slightly hooked nose. He stopped to have a word with the minister just inside the churchyard, then came out and mounted a fine black horse. He was about to ride off when he saw a dark little man coming out at the tail end of the rest.

'I am surprised you had the effrontery to show your face here today!' the man on the horse said in a loud harsh voice.

'He was my friend as well as your cousin,' said the man.

'And an evil influence you were upon him. At least now your machinations will come to naught!'

'By God, sir, if it were not such a solemn occasion I would fight you.'

'I would not fight with such as you, except to mow you down in battle,' said the other scornfully, and he trotted away, followed by most of the other mourners. The cart also creaked away, leaving me and the little man by the gate.

'Sir,' I said, 'am I right in thinking that was Sir James Freke who left just now?'

'It was, the worse for me,' he replied.

'And you have just buried his cousin, George Godwin, I take

it?'

'Yes, did you know him?'

'No, but I have an interest in his death. I am an apothecary of Dorchester, and have been told that he died of witchcraft. Is that true, do you think?'

'That is what is said. It was a most unfortunate death for us.'

'Who do you mean by "us"?'

'Look, sir, I do not know you. You're from Dorchester? Which side are you on in these wars?'

'King and Parliament,' I said guardedly. 'I wish for peace, and the King to rule with a free Parliament.'

'We all wish that,' he said, 'but what if the King will not have it? What if he brings in reinforcements through Weymouth to beat down Parliament and destroy it? What if he brings in more heathen Irish, as he did last November? What if he replenishes his munitions, as he did in February? What if papistical French troops pour in and conquer us and seek to destroy true religion, as they are like to do? Where will you stand then?'

'For England's freedom, I hope,' I said. 'If he brings in the French all true-hearted Englishmen will fight them, I should think!'

'No, sir,' he said. 'It will be too late if they are already landed; and not all will fight them—Sir James for one. There are those who are so blinded by the sparkle of the crown that they would accept even French oppression if it would keep the crown on the king's head.'

'Well, I am not one of those,' I said. 'I was distressed when Dorchester surrendered to the Cavaliers under Prince Maurice last year, and equally so when you in Melcombe and Weymouth did the same.'

He grasped my hand.

'You are a man after my own heart,' he said. 'I wonder... Tell me again why you have come.'

'As I said, a old man has been accused of witchcraft and of causing Mr Godwin's death, but I think this death may have been brought about by some other means. I have just been to the old man's cottage. It has been wrecked, and his furniture destroyed. And his cat.'

My words had a visible effect on the little man. He brightened and stood on tip-toe.

'The cat—what about a cat?'

'The cat is dead'

'"And the dog returns to his vomit".' He grasped my hand again. 'My dear sir, I never thought... But of course—your coming here to the funeral—you hoped perhaps to make contact. You must come to Melcombe, sir, and meet Nathaniel Webb, who is now our leader in name as well as fact. This unfortunate death of George Godwin, however it was caused, and the betrayal of secrets, has thrown us off course. But come what may we are determined to go through with it.'

I did not understand what he was talking about, but hoped still to learn more about what might lie behind Mr Godwin's death, so I humoured him.

'I will come with you some of the way, at anyrate,' I said, 'but is it safe? I've been told that the Cavaliers of the garrison are not a danger now, but I don't want to risk losing my horse.'

'It will be all right,' he said. 'It is not like when they first came, and didn't care what they did or how much they were hated as long as they secured the place. But when the Prince moved on and left a garrison things weren't so bad. The garrison have settled down now, made friends with the local girls and so on. All they want is to live comfortably and not be ordered elsewhere to fight and die. So they don't, I think, want to make the townspeople hate them for stealing and robbing. But anyway, most of them are across in Weymouth, in the Chapel Fort or up at Sandsfoot Castle.'

I was glad to have the groom's opinion confirmed by someone from the town, and agreed to go with him, thinking, indeed, that I would find out as much as he could tell me about Mr Godwin's affairs, and particularly his relations with his cousin, and then perhaps I would turn for home. So I began to walk beside him, leading my horse.

'Tell me,' I said, 'how was it that Mr Godwin was buried so quickly? Did the coroner sit to enquire how he died?'

'No he did not,' he replied. 'Sir James arranged the funeral, and I doubt if he so much as informed the coroner. He seemed to feel that a death by witchcraft was particularly disgraceful, and did not want it widely known.'

'The facts will have to come out if there is a trial, unless that too is hurried and the truth suppressed. But would you say that Sir James and his cousin were close, I mean as friends?'

'They certainly seemed to meet often. But I thought of George Godwin as my friend, for he told us that he couldn't stand his cousin's blind adherence to the King's party. In fact, as you probably know, we called him our leader, though Webb has really kept us together. But tell me, sir, how are you doing in Dorchester? Since Godwin's last report we have heard nothing. You have not such a large garrison of Cavaliers as we do, I believe. Do you think they will be easily overcome when the day arrives?'

'With outside help I expect so,' I said, beginning to guess his drift.

'Undoubtedly, that will be needed of course,' he said, 'and that is what Godwin was trying to arrange before his so unfortunate death. He had made certain plans with your Mr Barton, but we do not know exactly what they were, so your coming is providential. The Lord, having afflicted us, is now looking upon us with favour again. How fortunate it was that Godwin had arranged the passwords, otherwise we might not have known one another.'

I felt that Obadiah Horner was drawing me into some plot that I did not fully understand, and that I was in danger of getting into deeper water than I could swim in. But I had not yet found out all he might tell me about Mr Godwin.

'If he was so much for the Cause,' I ventured, 'I'm surprised that he should visit his cousin, if Sir James is as rabid a Cavalier as you say.'

'Ah, that was his subtlety,' he replied. 'George wanted Sir James to find out the dispositions and numbers of the garrison, and any future movements of troops, and what other forces might come this way, and to pass on the information to him. Sir James is well known to the Governor and often dines with him.'

'What has made Mr Godwin's death so particularly unsettling just now? I heard Sir James say, "Your machinations will come to naught"—how much did he know?'

'He may have known, indeed he must have known, that there are a lot of us in Melcombe and Weymouth who want to get rid of the garrison and return our towns to Parliament. He would know, too, that such a coup would perhaps be the decisive action in this war, for Weymouth is the only port the King still holds on the south coast. No doubt he plans to bring in armaments and those French troops I mentioned, which could finally swing the battle his way. But if he loses Weymouth he will lose the war. I fear some information about our plans has been passed to the Governor. I hope, though, that he does not know exactly how far we have progressed, and how near we are to taking action. As you know, George Godwin was both our leader and our link with Dorchester, but he also had many excellent ideas about how we could proceed, so his death is a big loss to the Cause, besides being the loss of a friend.'

I began to feel that Mr Horner could not be so unbalanced as I had imagined if he could set out the position so sensibly, though I suspected him of exaggerating the effect the loss of Weymouth would have upon the King's prospects. Perhaps these conspirators were not such a mad-cap group as I had thought at first. My curiosity got the better of my discretion, and I determined to find out more.

Chapter 4 Plotters

AS MR HORNER was small I felt my horse could carry both of us with ease, so suggested that he should ride pillion. I mounted and he scrambled up behind, and we went along at a steady walk. At the place where on an earlier visit I had passed a sentry post I saw no soldiers, and when I remarked on this Mr Horner said:

'They're not often here now. No doubt if they thought an attack was likely, or knew that someone was coming whom they wished to stop, they would post sentries here. But we shall easily overpower them if they are here when the Day comes.'

I supposed he must be referring to some rising being planned by his group of Roundheads. Evidently he thought I would know all about it and, without letting him realise that I did not, I tried to probe further.

'Will all be ready for the Day?' I asked.

'We're certainly not ready yet, and Godwin's death has caused some difficulty. Mr Webb will have much to discuss with you, I have no doubt,' he replied. I felt Mr Nathaniel Webb would discover my ignorance all too soon, and might suspect me of being a fraud, or worse, a spy. But we were now entering the outskirts of Melcombe, and it seemed too late to turn back.

Mr Horner directed me to one of the back streets, and into a yard where I could leave my horse near a stone water-trough. Then he led me up some worn slate steps and knocked at a door, two knocks, then two more.

It was opened by a giant of a man who looked like a wrestler or prize-fighter. He had close-cropped hair and black bristles on his chin which had not been shaved for a day or two. He was in his shirt sleeves, and his arm muscles bulged as thick as a normal man's legs. He scowled at us for a moment without speaking, then said:

'Who's this?'

'It's all right, Ted,' said Mr Horner, 'he's one of us.'

The big man half turned to call behind him, while still blocking the doorway.

'Mr Horner's brought a stranger. Shall I let 'im in?'

There was a movement inside, and a short man of about thirty years of age, with a very round head, a little black beard and greasy black hair over his ears, looked out beside the giant.

'Ah, Obadiah,' he said, without much warmth, 'who have you got there?'

'This is Mr Judd of Dorchester,' Obadiah answered. 'He was at the funeral, but I didn't know him, of course, until he gave the password.'

'Which word did he give?'

'"The cat is dead".'

'"And the dog returns to his vomit", good, good' he said in a more welcoming tone. 'Right, Magog, let them in.' The giant stood back and we entered and he held out his hand. 'Come in, Mr Judd, you will be able to tell us how the brothers in Dorchester are doing. Mr Barton sent you, I suppose?'

I had to think quickly. Should I confess that I was not a member of any group of conspirators? I had almost decided to do so, but the giant behind still breathing suspiciously down my neck made me hesitate, especially when I saw what looked like his twin standing at the other side of the room. Magog, or Ted, slouched over to the other, and they stood looking at me as if wondering which part to break first. Both stood with their arms folded, and both had ugly faces, huge muscles and, with their cropped heads bent forward, reminded me of a couple of mastiffs. The second one had a broken nose which made him seem even worse. Both looked as if they could kill a man without effort and without compunction. If I confessed now what would they do to me? If I was to get away unharmed I would have to pretend I was one of the plotters.

The man with the long chin must have noticed my hesitation.

'Don't worry about our friends,' he said. 'They are only dangerous to our enemies. I call them Gog and Magog. I, by the way, am Nathaniel Webb, of whom you've no doubt heard.'

I shook his hand.

'I have indeed heard of you, Mr Webb,' I said, not confessing that I had only heard of him from Mr Horner in the last half hour. 'It is an honour to meet you.'

He warmed further at that, and invited me to sit down at a table, and asked Obadiah to fetch some ale.'

'Now, Mr Judd,' he said, 'it is surely the Lord's doing that you have come just now, because we were wondering what to do. George Godwin had been in touch with Mr Barton, but was killed before he could tell us all that had been arranged, but I suppose you know all about it?'

'Not so,' I said, desperately hoping I would not reveal my total ignorance. 'I am really just a messenger. I came to find out what I could about George Godwin's death. Was he really killed by witchcraft, or was it because someone had found out about the plot? But if you can tell me how things stand now, I could convey to Mr Barton anything you wish.'

'But didn't Mr Barton have a reply to our question?'

'I have not been sent with a message,' I said. 'Are you sure Mr Godwin asked Mr Barton?'

'No I am not,' he said in a low tone, and looking over his shoulder added, 'Obadiah does not know it, but I suspect that Godwin was a traitor.'

'How do you mean?' I asked.

'I'll tell you later,' he said, as Obadiah came back with the ale, and sat down with us at the table. 'Now, Mr Judd, if you haven't brought a message, explain why have you come here to me?'

'I went to the funeral to inquire (as I said) about Mr Godwin and his death and, as your friend has explained, we met and he invited me here.'

'Then you were not on your way to us?' Mr Webb gave me a

hard stare.

'As I've told you, I was trying to find out what had really happened to Mr Godwin, and what were the implications of his death for us in Dorchester. It was fortuitous that I met Mr Horner; but it has worked out very well, for here I am.'

'Can you at least take a message back to Mr Barton?'

'Oh yes,' I said, 'I can see him as soon as I get back to Dorchester. What do you want me to say?'

'Our immediate problem, Mr Judd,' said Webb, 'as you may know, is how to get in touch with the Earl of Essex, and that is what I hoped Mr Barton would help us with.'

'But surely that can be arranged without difficulty,' I said.

'Can you arrange it? Do you have a messenger ready, who knows where the Earl is and who would have access to him?'

'Yes, we have someone who could go for us,' I said, wondering why this should be such a problem, 'but have you got a message ready for the Earl?'

'That is the next problem,' said Mr Webb.

'—and where we feel the loss of George Godwin so much,' said Mr Horner breaking in. 'He would have known how to put the message in the right way. He had a gift with words, as you may remember, and would surely have composed a letter which would have persuaded the Earl. You see, Mr Judd, as I'm sure you know, the Earl of Essex is the only man who is trusted enough by our people here to give them the courage to risk their lives in a rising.'

'That is the difficulty,' said Webb, 'if we are ever to throw off the pestilential yoke of bondage we suffer under, we must have a large Parliamentary force come here, and it must be commanded by Essex. No one else will do.'

'How will you hold the place if Essex then moves on?' I asked. 'The trouble in so many places has been that it is comparatively easy for our troops to throw out the Cavaliers, but as soon as they go the Cavaliers come back.'

'Here we have Chapel Fort and Sandsfoot Castle, and the river and the marshes to defend us. If we once get control we shall not easily give it up,' said Webb firmly.

'So how are you going to persuade Essex to come?' I asked.

'We hoped Mr Barton would have ideas about that. Did he really say nothing about it for you to tell us?'

'Have you writing materials here?' I said, playing for time. 'Let us draft a letter now. You can point out to the Earl the importance of Weymouth to the King, and that if he, that is Essex, comes you will raise the town against the garrison, open the gates, and hand him a glorious victory.'

'And remind him of the supplies the Cavaliers are bringing in through this port,' added Obadiah.

'And of the danger of French soldiers landing,' I said.

'Yes, yes,' cried Webb, leaping to his feet, 'this will surely be a bait to catch him with. I'll get paper and ink.'

He was soon back with the writing materials and Obadiah acted as scribe.

'We should begin,' he said, '"To the right worshipful the Earl of Essex".'

'Go on,' I suggested, '"Honoured Sir, we your humble petitioners of Melcombe and Weymouth, invite you to come to our aid".'

'Put it more strongly,' said Webb, 'put "beg you".'

'I'll put "beseech you",' said Obadiah.

And so we went on until the letter was finished. Obadiah then read it out:

To the right worshipful the Earl of Essex.

Honoured Sir,

We your humble petitioners of Melcombe and Weymouth beseech you to come to our aid.

The king has already landed munitions and Irish soldiery here, and is ere long most likely to bring in a horde of the French, to the utter ruin of Parliament, unless you speedily regain our towns.

We are ready to overpower the garrison and open the gates to you, Sir, if you will but come with a sufficient army. None but you, Sir, can give us the confidence to do this, but if you come you will have an extraordinary triumph and strike terror to the enemy.

We respectfully await your reply by this messenger,
and have the honour to remain, Sir,
your humble and faithful petitioners.

'Write it out fair,' said Webb to Obadiah. 'I will have a word with Mr Judd in the next room.' He led me past the 'mastiffs', signing for them to follow, and led us into the small room adjoining. One of the guards shut the door, and they stood close behind me.

'Mr Judd,' he said, wheeling about abruptly, 'I know nothing about you, and for all I know you may be a spy. Who are you?'

'I've told you,' I said, 'I am truly Micah Judd, an apothecary of Dorchester, and I am not a spy.'

'Why are you inquiring about George Godwin's death?'

'His death is surely very important for all of us. It might mean that the plot is known and we are betrayed. But I have an additional reason for making enquiries, as I explained to Mr Horner. A man I know has been accused of murdering him. I believe the man is innocent, so I am hoping to find out how he really died.'

'I would not enquire too closely if I were you.'

'Why not?'

'As I told you, I had reason to believe that Godwin was a traitor. Traitors die. So see that you do not betray us. Godwin was one of us, so I thought. But he was too close to that cousin of his, and was, I fear, playing a double game. Either by carelessness or design some our plans have become known to the enemy. So you see what has happened to the man who knew too much. Do I make myself clear?'

'No,' I said. 'Are you telling me that you killed Mr Godwin for betraying you?'

'I am telling you nothing,' he said, 'merely warning you to remember Godwin if you are ever tempted to do the same. I am still troubled that you did not come here with a message from Barton.'

'No, but I will faithfully carry your letter back.'

'Swear it.'

'I swear it,' I said.

'Look behind you, Mr Judd.'

I turned and saw the two guards standing so close I could smell their breath.

'Gog and Magog have each killed their man,' said Webb calmly. 'If you so much as think of betraying us remember them—and remember Godwin. That is all, Mr Judd. You need say nothing of this to Obadiah. Let him continue to think of Godwin as a martyr to the Cause.'

He ushered me back into the other room, where Obadiah was writing carefully with the tip of his tongue peeping from the corner of his mouth. When he was done he and Webb both signed the letter, and the latter told one of the guards to bring a candle which, when it was brought and lit, he used to melt some sealing wax. After he had pressed his ring into the seal he handed me the letter and I tucked it into my doublet and prepared to leave.

'How will you get it to the Earl?' asked Webb.

'Do you know where he is?' Obadiah added.

'No matter,' I said, 'leave it to me. As I told you just now, I have someone in mind who will be an excellent messenger to take it safely, and find the Earl.'

'Is he reliable? Is he to be trusted?' asked Webb.

'Absolutely,' I said, 'have no fears. But how can I find you to pass on the reply, if it comes?'

'You may come here,' said Webb.

'That may not be safe or convenient,' I said. 'There must be a surer way.' I considered for a moment.

'Perhaps we could meet again at Radipole,' suggested Horner.

But I shook my head.

'I know,' I said, 'I will send you a package of pills with the reply wrapped in it. I can send it by the tranter.' (That is by the carrier, who goes from Dorchester to Weymouth once a week or so.) 'In case it falls into the wrong hands I will devise the message as if it refers to medicines. I will call Lord Essex "the doctor", and let you know when he expects to visit "the patient"—that is Weymouth. But also if need be you can get in touch with me at my apothecary's shop in Durn Lane, Dorchester.'

They agreed, and I shook hands with them, then went down into the yard and mounted my horse. As I rode away I saw the two 'mastiffs' had come out to the top of the stairs and were looking at me unsmiling. I raised my hand to them, but they did not respond, and I certainly breathed more easily when I was out of their sight.

As I rode I wondered what sort of a mess I had got myself into. I had not found out enough to mount an effective defence for Malachy, and the suspicions I had begun to form of Sir James's part in the death of Godwin had been upset by what Mr Webb had said. He had hinted that Godwin's death had been a punishment, yet he had not absolutely confessed to having done the deed himself. Although he suspected Godwin of treachery, his death could still have been from natural causes, and Webb simply using it to make me fear to betray their plotting.

Certainly, he had made me aware of the risks I was running. I had become involved in a dangerous intrigue with men I scarcely knew but who themselves seemed dangerous. If the latest plot became known to the Cavaliers I might be punished along with the other conspirators. Even if it were kept secret I could well believe that Mr Webb would not stick at murder. If he found out that I was not one of the Dorchester group of plotters my life would not be worth much. I decided I had better make myself known to Mr Barton and persuade him that I was fit to join his people, even if I did not become fully one of them.

I rode over the ridge and down the gentle slope to Dorchester, thinking rather sadly of how important Weymouth seemed compared with Dorchester. Before Dorchester surrendered to the Royalists I had thought it a key place, guarding as it did the roads north from the coast and east and west. But now it did not seem to matter much to the success of either side, whereas Weymouth, though perhaps not as crucial as Obadiah thought, was a vital port. Dorchester hadn't been fought over even as much as little Wareham, but perhaps (thought I) that was a blessing and why Dorchester was a good place to live.

I was somewhat surprised to have discovered that Mr Barton was attempting actually to do something for the Parliamentary Cause as well as merely abusing his opponents. And the thought that such a man, whom I had before considered rather a fool, should be so active for Parliament made me feel that I myself ought to do more. I had been angry and frustrated that our efforts in Dorchester had been so feeble, and I remembered rather sadly how much I had wanted to do for the Parliamentary Cause a few months before. I had become disillusioned, even a bit cynical, but now was a chance to take some action. By the time I reached Dorchester I had quite persuaded myself that I would be doing right to be more involved.

Although I was going to see Mr Barton, I planned to send the letter by my own messenger rather than his, for I was sure I knew just the person to get it to the Earl successfully. So after I had rubbed down my horse and settled him with food and water, and had eaten with my wife, I went to find Mr Barton, whose house was at the far end of South Street.

His maidservant showed me into a small room or closet which Mr Barton evidently used as a study. There were two chairs, a cupboard, a few books mainly of sermons on a shelf, a desk, and a framed text on the wall: *Thou God seest me.*

Mr Barton entered and shook hands; a somewhat slow-moving heavy man with pink jowls.

'Don't I know ye?' he said. 'I think I have seen ye somewhere in the town.'

'I'm Micah Judd, the apothecary, from Durn Lane,' I said.

'Ah yes, I remember. And to what do I owe this visit, Mr Judd?'

'I think you and I may be working in the same business.'

'I don't understand. I have nothing to do with apothecaries nor, as far as I am aware, with you.'

'If I said "The cat is dead" would it mean anything to you?'

'"And the dog is returned to his vomit", by the Lord!—If you are one of us how is it that I haven't known?'

'I have only recently become involved. But I was in Melcombe today, and met some of our people there. You know, I expect, that George Godwin is dead?'

'I had heard it, and by witchcraft, I believe. The Evil One is indeed fighting against us. If the devil is trying so to frustrate us it must surely mean that we are doing the Lord's work.'

'I am not convinced that his death was by witchcraft. I have been making inquiries and trying to find out more about it. It seems that there were several people who might have wanted to have him out of the way. And you, sir, do you know of anyone who might have had reason to kill him?'

'No, I can't say that I do. But witchcraft is Satan's work and dangerous to all who dabble in it. The Scriptures also warn us against it, so have nothing to do with it and its results, Mr Judd, that is my advice.'

'But if Mr Godwin was murdered by some other means...?'

'I suppose someone who opposed what he was doing might have tried to remove him. But his work was secret, and few knew of it.'

'His cousin is a strong Cavalier.'

'I know nothing of him. I only know that Mr Godwin was a godly member—the leader in fact—of our people in Melcombe and Weymouth, and that he was working to ensure that any action we took here could be worked in with whatever was afoot in Weymouth.'

'Well, I hope you will include me in your plans here,' I said.

'How far can I trust you?' he pondered.

'It seems to me that you will have to trust me,' I said, 'seeing I have been accepted by our friends in Weymouth and have been entrusted with their letter.'

'What letter is this?'

'How far can *I* trust *you?*' I said.

He made a somewhat sour face.

'It seems we must trust each other,' he said.

I seized his hand again in mine, saying:

'Done! Let us be open with one another. You know Mr Webb's seal, I expect.' I took out the letter and showed him the seal, then turned it over for him to see that it was addressed to Lord Essex. 'We must not break it open, but I will tell you what it contains, and then perhaps you can tell me how far your plans have progressed here.'

'Well, what does the letter say?'

'It is from both Mr Webb and Mr Horner, do you know them both?'

'Only Mr Webb, but I have heard him mention Mr Horner.'

'They write to remind Lord Essex that the King has already brought in munitions and troops through Weymouth, and will bring in a deadly force of Frenchmen unless the port is secured for Parliament. Their letter urges him to come, and promises that then the people will rise and let him in and give him a great victory. They believe that only Lord Essex will be trusted enough by the people to give them the resolution to risk a rising, so they are appealing very strongly for the Earl to come in person.'

'I think they are probably right in that, but I also think it is very doubtful that he will come, occupied as he is in other parts of England. And how are we to get this letter to him?—it could be difficult.''

'Why so? There must be someone who could take it to him.'

'I fear I cannot at this moment think of anyone we could send. I wonder who would go on such a mission? Would you go? I don't even know where the Earl is at present.'

'I cannot go myself,' I said, 'but I believe I may be able to arrange a trusty messenger. But tell me, if the Earl does come will you be ready for him?'

'We have plans to strike at our enemies, but they are not very far advanced as yet. We have the names of twenty or thirty townsmen who will (I hope) do their part when the moment comes. What I intend is, when the time is ripe we will take Churchill and Paty and Haggard and some others of their party into custody. I would hope that then we will so strengthen the resolve of the people here that we would be able to let the Earl (or whichever of our Parliament generals comes) enter without trouble, and afterwards hold the town for Parliament.'

I felt a bit disappointed. It sounded to me as if a lot of his 'plans' were still far too vague and largely wishful thinking. However I tried to sound pleased.

'That will be a great thing if you can bring it about, and believe me, Mr Barton, I shall be glad to do my part. I will go and see about the letter now, and meanwhile there are two things I would ask of you.'

'Yes?'

'First, please would you let me know when your plans are further advanced, so that I can do my part for the Cause. And secondly, if our friends in Weymouth get in touch with you please would you let them know that I have sent the letter.'

He agreed to do what I asked, and himself ushered me to the door.

'You mentioned Mr Haggard as someone to be arrested,' I said as he opened it. 'I know he is a staunch Royalist, but he has an excellent daughter, and for her sake I would hope he might be spared.'

'He is an enemy of right government and true religion,' said Mr Barton with some heat. 'His daughter may be as fair as Bathsheba and as virtuous as Ruth wife of Boaz, but with such a father I want no connection with her.'

As I had not mentioned such a connection I took it that his son's wish to marry Rachel Haggard was still a very sore point for him, and that any further word from me on the subject would hinder rather than help them, so I wished him good evening and left.

It was now about seven o' clock, and I was tired after all the events of the day. Nevertheless I steeled myself for one more thing, and walked up to Top o' Town and out of West Gate and the mile or so to Wolfeton House.

The Trenchards were still away, but Lady Alicia was there as I hoped, and I was soon led up the grand staircase to a long gallery where she was pacing to and fro. There were old family portraits on the walls and rush matting on the floor. The Lady turned as I entered and her face lit up.

'Mr Judd, the apothecary!' she exclaimed. 'What brings you here, so late too?'

'When I saw you the other day, my lady, you said you wished you were a man and could fight.'

'I did, I still do. I am tired of spending my life here waiting for something to happen.'

'Then I may be able to help you,' I said, 'if you are willing to travel.'

'Don't talk in riddles, sir,' she said. 'If it's something for Parliament that I can do to hit these arrogant Cavaliers, I'll do it.'

'I have a letter for the Earl of Essex, and it is most important that it reaches him as soon as possible. I remember you said you know him?'

'Uncle Robert, yes of course, my father campaigned with him in Germany when he first went to war.'

'Is he then your uncle, my lady?'

'I call him Uncle, though he is no relation really, and he's always been kind to me when we've met. Is this letter so very important?'

'Yes, my lady, it could make a vital difference to the Parliament Cause. You see, the King is trying to get reinforcements from

France—he hopes the French troops, with their experience of fighting in the continental wars, will swing the balance in the war here. But for them to land safely he needs control of a port, preferably on the south coast, and at the moment Weymouth is the place—the one place he holds.'

'I understand that. In fact I have been surprised that our leaders on the Parliament side have not sent sent forces to drive out the Cavaliers. But I suppose they are too occupied with watching the king. But can you tell me what this letter is about—and why you have come to me?'

'Indeed I can, my lady. The letter is from the leader of our people in Weymouth. I am sure I can trust you with his name, though it must not be noised abroad for obvious reasons. He is a Mr Webb, a very able man, who gave me the letter today. He is confident that he will be able to overcome the Cavalier garrison and hand Melcombe and Weymouth over to Parliament. But he can only achieve this if a Parliamentary general comes with sufficient forces to take over the towns and capture the castle—Sandsfoot, which is too strong for any but professional soldiers to capture.'

'How wonderful!' she exclaimed. 'But why are you telling me this?'

'Well, there is a problem, my lady. Mr Webb is afraid that the Weymouth people will only rise up against the Royalists if they have complete confidence in the Parliament general who comes, and he strongly believes that the only general they will really trust is the Earl of Essex. So this letter is an attempt to persuade Lord Essex to come. The hope is that he will be willing to time his attack in concert with the rising in the towns, so that in effect the conspirators will hand him the victory. The King's scheming with the French will be foiled, and Essex might then go on to relieve Lyme, which is holding out so bravely against Prince Maurice.'

'I see,' she said, her eyes sparkling,'it is a grand plan, and ought to succeed for its very boldness.'

'There is another thing,' I said.'This ought to be put in hand without delay, not only to prevent the French landing (and for all we know they may come at any time), but because there is danger of the plotters being betrayed. One has already died, probably killed, either because he was a traitor giving information to the Cavalier Governor, or because he was known to be a conspirator. There is a Sir James Freke of Upwey, who is a great enemy of our Cause. Do you know him?'

'No, I've heard of the Freke family, but I don't know Sir James.'

'I suspect him of working to destroy the planned uprising before it can take place, so the sooner things can be put in hand the better. So you see how important it is to get this letter to Lord Essex and persuade him to come.'

'And you want me...?' she said and paused, looking rather astonished.

'Yes, my lady. You could get through where a man might be stopped. Also you, knowing the Earl, will be able to have access to him, and could add your reasoning to the letter and persuade him.'

'I'm sure he would see me, if I could get to him. But I'm not at all sure where he is.'

'But you could surely find out?'

'I suppose so. Yes, of course I could—I could ride towards London and someone on the way would be sure to direct me.'

'Then you will go?' I asked.

'Yes, Mr Judd, I will go first thing tomorrow.' Her eyes seemed to dance. 'You have cheered me up. I was feeling so melancholy at not being able to do anything. But now already I begin to feel right well and happy.'

I handed her the letter and asked her to send me the Earl's reply as soon as she got back, so that I could pass it on to the Weymouth people. As I left I heard her calling to a servant:

'Tell Richard to have horses ready early tomorrow, and that he and Thomas are to come with me to London.'

Richard must be her groom, I supposed, and Thomas a trusted

retainer. Will they really be enough to defend her? I wondered. What if she meets a band of robbers? or is stopped and searched by the Cavaliers? Well, I thought with a shrug, the letter is now out of my hands, and I can only await events.

Chapter 5 Malachy and Matthew

THE FOLLOWING DAY being Lord's Day I went to St Peter's Church. The King's party were still strong in Dorchester, and the preacher was a Royalist chaplain, who read a rather dull sermon. It was about obeying 'the powers that be' from St Paul's Epistle to the Romans, chapter 13. But although the preacher drew from it the duty of submitting to the King, it struck me that the text might equally enjoin obedience to a lawfully established Parliament. Afterwards I walked down to the prison to visit Malachy. The Keeper seemed surprised to see me.

'You again!' he said. 'I thought you'd keep away from the witch, like most sensible Christian folk.'

'I don't accept that he is a witch,' I said, 'and you shouldn't call him such before he's found guilty.'

'He's a witch or wizard or he-witch, call him what you will,' he said. 'He's got the marks o' Satan, sure enough, no doubt about it.'

'He's still not guilty until declared so in a proper court of law,' I said angrily.

'He wouldn't be here if he wasn't guilty,' he retorted. But he accepted the coin I put in his hand, and led me along the passage.

'Your friend has got more company,' he said over his shoulder.

'Who is that?'

'Only a drunk,' he said. 'Took more than he could hold on Saturday night, and got picked up by the constables. Waste o' good money an' good liquor.'

He glanced through the grating and opened the door, and stood aside for me to enter. There I saw Malachy and his former companion, Robert Still—and the drunk who lay half propped against the wall in a corner, snoring and groaning. Robert looked at me warily, afraid perhaps that I would blame him for Malachy's state. The latter was sitting on the bench gazing at his feet, looking the picture of utter dejection, uncared for and careless of himself and his surroundings. He did not move or look up as I approached him.

'Mr Moore,' I said, 'it is I, Micah Judd.'

I touched his arm and he slowly lifted his head and looked at me for a moment, then looked down at the floor again.

'I've been to Upwey to your home as I promised,' I said.

'Upwey, aye,' he said dully, as if it was no concern of his.

'I visited your cottage, and...' I hesitated, wondering how to tell him about his cat. But he showed signs of interest at last.

'Simmany?' he asked, looking up, 'Simmany, did you find 'un?'

'I did, and, Mr Moore, I am so very sorry...'

'He's dead, isn' he?

'I'm afraid so. I found him dead in the house, and buried him in your garden.'

He put his hands over his face, and suddenly his tears began to flow. He gave a cry like that of an animal in pain and rocked to and fro.

'Simmany, poor ol' Simmany,' he said at last, and then great sobs again shook his whole body. I almost felt like crying in sympathy, and even Robert Still looked downcast and wiped his sleeve across his eyes.

After a time Malachy became calmer. He too wiped his eyes and but didn't look up.

'Thank 'ee, zur, for burying 'un,' he said. 'I don't s'pose I shall ever see his grave, but thank 'ee all the same. I expect you wonder at me grievin' for a cat, but he was a real friend, was Simmany, an' he knew—oh, there was hardly a thing he didn' know.'

'I'm sorry,' I said. 'But don't tell anyone else how much he meant to you, for they might try to make out that he was your familiar spirit, given you by Satan.'

I caught sight of Robert Still with a peculiar crafty expression on his face, but he turned away when I looked at him.

'I also asked around in the village, trying to find out more about Mr Godwin's death,' I went on. 'It seems to me much more likely that it was caused by poison than by your curses, but whether it was an accident, and he ate something that disagreed with him, or whether some enemy murdered him, I don't know. Do you know of anyone apart from you who had reason to hate him?'

'It was me curse that killed him,' said Malachy.

'Nonsense, you must not say that' I said firmly, though in spite of my earlier reasoning I felt a shiver of dread, like I had after visiting his cottage. 'Tell me, Malachy, give me your solemn word in truth, have you ever made a pact with the devil and sold your soul to Satan?'

He paused long before answering.

'The truth, now,' I said.

'I daun' rightly know,' he said slowly. 'Where do my powers come from, the power o' the hazel rod, if not from him down below? Passon do say they come from Satan.'

'What does your parson know about it? Your gifts may well come from your Maker, perhaps, that is from God. Doesn't the Bible say that He is the giver of all good gifts? But you haven't answered my question: Have you ever made a pact or bargain with the devil?'

'No, zur,' he said firmly, 'I never done that. I've been called a devil time an' again, but I've had no truck wi' him, I've never made any bargain wi' him. But are you saying the power o' my cusses came from Him up aloft an' not from him down below?

'I'm saying your curse, wherever it came from, didn't have the power to kill and it didn't kill George Godwin.'

'But it did, zur. It happened as I said: I cussed him an' he died.'

'You silly man,' I cried, exasperated by his stupid obstinacy, 'if you say that, you'll surely be condemned to die. If you renounce the devil and any thought that you caused Mr Godwin's death, and if we can prove what really caused it, you might be found not guilty. But if you give them any excuse to call you a witch you'll die.'

'They'll kill me sure enough,' he said, 'like they killed my Simmany.' He brushed away another tear.

'But they haven't yet proved you a witch, have they?'

'How do they prove a witch?' he said. 'They drown you—unless you float, and then you're a witch. Or they ask whose cow isn't givin' milk, or whose milk's not turnin' to butter, or whose chile's havin' fits, an' that proves you're a witch. Or they come an' stick pins in you and see if you bleed, or they search your body for warts and such. See here —' He pulled open his shirt and showed my a brown spot near his left nipple—'they've seen that, an' they say that proves I'm a witch. Who's ever been let off, once a body's been accused o' being a witch, eh?'

He sank back against the wall and buried his face in his hands.

'But have they examined you? Have they given you tests for witchcraft?'

'Ay, zur, that they have. I daun' know which day it were, when a minister came an' axed me all sorts o' questions.'

'What about?'

'Oh, 'bout the devil an' what he looked like, an' how I called 'un up, an' whether I suckled 'un. All kinds o' rummage.'

'What did you answer?'

'I kep' quiet mostly. I told 'un I didn' understand what he was talkin' about.'

'That was probably the best thing to do,' I said. 'Do you know who he was?'

'No, zur, they didn' tell me his name.'

'Did he do anything else, or just ask you questions?'

'They made me take all me clothes off, an' the keeper held me down while the passon searched me for signs o' the devil.'

'Did he claim to have found any?'

'As I told you, they found this spot on me front, an' he said it was a devil's nipple. They said they found another behind, and then they stuck pins into me, an' sometimes they hurt—by'r lady they did!—an' sometimes when they said they'd stuck me I didn' feel a thing.'

'Maybe then they were only pretending to stick you,' I said.

'I daun' know, zur. I only know what they did say.'

'And it was just this minister and the gaol-keeper doing all this?'

'Them two. They let me put me things on then, an' brought me back here. An' I tell you, zur, I daun' want to go through that again! But they said I have the marks o' the Evil One.'

'Don't believe them,' I said. 'Many people have marks on their bodies, but that doesn't mean they've had dealings with Satan.'

'I daun' know what to say,' he said doubtfully.

'Don't help your enemies,' I said firmly. 'Don't admit anything, certainly don't say your curses caused Godwin's death, don't admit to having anything to do with Satan.'

'All I cared for was Simmany, an' he's dead,' he said quietly.

'Well, you maintain your innocence for Simmany's sake,' I said. 'If they say you're a witch they'll say Simmany was possessed by the devil, and you mustn't let them. Give me your word now that you'll say you're not guilty, and have had no dealings at all with Satan. Will you promise?'

''Twon't make no difference,' he said. 'They're not going to let me go, whatever anyone do say.'

'You mustn't give up hope so easily,' I urged him. But he only shook his head and looked at the ground.'At least think about what I've said.' I laid my hand on his shoulder, and could feel him shrink at the touch. Perhaps it reminded him of the ill-treatment he had recently suffered at the hands of the minister and gaol-keeper.

'I must leave you now,' I said, 'but I will come and see you again.'

He looked up at last and grasped my hand for a moment.

'Thank 'ee, zur, for what you did for Simmany,' he said, and buried his face again.

As I banged on the door and called through the grating to be let out, the drunk stirred and opened his eyes, belched loudly and was sick all down his front.

When we reached the outer door I said to the keeper, 'Mr Moore says you have examined him for signs of witchcraft. Was this a properly authorised examination? Who was with you?'

'It was right enough,' he said. 'The minister who's now at All Saints church was sent along here by the magistrates, and he and I examined him together. It was all done according to the proper form, an' he'll bear witness to the same.'

'What did you find?'

'Oh arrh,' he said, 'he's a witch, sure 'nuff. I told you, he has the marks o' Satan, no question.'

'But you surely cannot believe that a wart or a pimple is a devil's mark! I warrant that most people—yourself included—have some odd marks or spots on the body. They prove nothing.'

'You get out, Mr Apothecary,' he said rudely. 'Folk do take note that you be calling on the witch, so you'd best take care. When he comes to trial I shall testify to what I've seen an' heard.'

'Don't you threaten me, man,' I said. 'Mr Moore hasn't been found guilty yet, and until he is—if he is—you and I must presume he's innocent. But let us not quarrel,' I added, for I did not want the keeper either to hinder my seeing Malachy or to make his treatment worse. 'You are doing your duty, I know, and my only concern is that he should not suffer if he is not guilty.'

'I'll not make him suffer, that'll be work for the hangman. He'll suffer no more at my hands than any other prisoner, witch or no witch.' he said somewhat haughtily, 'But I tell you, sir, I'd rather have an adulterer or a murderer in my charge than a witch.'

'I'm sure you would,' I said, 'but have no fear—he hasn't harmed me, and I'm sure he won't harm you.'

I shook his hand. I disliked doing so, and a great meaty hand it was, but for Malachy's sake I wanted the Keeper to think of me as a friend. But I was worried, wondering whether the poor old man would survive until his trial, he seemed so to be sinking. I did not know what more to do for him, and in view of his probable fate it might be best for him to die in prison.

Next morning a young fellow entered my shop and introduced himself as Matthew Barton. I could see his father's likeness in his eyes and chin, but his manners (I was pleased to find) were quite different. He was dressed in dark clothes in the Puritan style, yet had a coloured feather in his hat which seemed to declare, 'I may dress soberly to please my father, but in my head I have my own thoughts!' He came in quietly and gave a curious stare at my shelves of bottles and phials, and the bench on which were a couple of bowls and my pestle and mortar.

'What can I do for you?' I asked.

'I, er... I don't want any medicines. I wondered... that is, Rachel had a talk with you the other day, Rachel Haggard, that is. She said you were helpful to her.'

He went bright red to the roots of his light brown hair.

'I'm glad of that,' I said, 'for I wasn't able to give her what she wanted. She wondered if I had a medicine which would change people's minds, but I told her the only way to do that is by patience, to let time bring them around.'

'She told you that she and I... ?'

'...That you and she want to marry, but that your fathers disapprove, yes.'

'I wondered, do you know either of them? My father is very firm for Parliament and yesterday I heard him mention you among those he thought would support the Roundhead cause. Do you know him, sir?'

'Oddly enough, although until recently I don't think I ever exchanged a word with him, I went to see him a couple of days ago, and thinking of what Rachel had said, I mentioned her to him as a fine girl. His angry response made me understand that anything else I might have been thinking of saying would not be helpful. So, if you have a mind to ask me to put in a word for you, I don't think it would do any good. You are right, though, that in general I would agree with your father and incline to Parliament, though not (I suspect) as fervently as he does.'

'What about Rachel's father, Mr Haggard? Do you have any dealings with him?'

'I'm afraid not, though if chance were to make our paths cross, I would try to say something good on your behalf.'

'Thank you, sir, I can't ask more.'

'But I don't think anything I said would have much weight from what I've heard of him, especially if he happens to be aware that I incline to what he thinks is the wrong party.'

'No, there's not much hope then.'

'But do remember what I told Rachel, that "things do come around". Be patient and you may well get what you want. After all, who knows what twists the war may take, and who will be governing Dorchester in six months time?'

'I'm afraid if the war comes near to us again it will set my father and Mr Haggard more at odds than ever.'

'Perhaps so, perhaps not,' I said. 'Meanwhile, my advice is, be a dutiful son as far as you can, and don't give either your father or Mr Haggard reason to blame you, apart from your love for Rachel.'

'You don't really know what my father's like. Oh, I know you've met him, but you can't know what he's like at home. He's so set against those he disagrees with, he won't listen to anything on the other side,' he said ruefully. 'I will try to do as you say. But father thinks I'm a traitor to Parliament for even thinking of wooing a Cavalier's daughter.'

Then as he still didn't leave, but gazed around the shop, I said: 'Are you interested in my art?'

'Pardon me, sir,' he said, blushing again, 'I have never been in an apothecary's shop before. I was wondering what all these bottles and things are for.'

'There are dried herbs in most of the wide-topped jars, and some wrapped in brown paper,' I said, 'and conserves, oils, syrups, various ointments in some of the bottles. Different plants have different virtues, and sometimes the virtue is only in a part of the plant—the seeds or roots or flowers or leaves.'

'Does each disease have a plant that can cure it?'

'Would that it were that simple,' I said with a laugh. 'As you will know, there are four humours or elements which govern each person's body and mind, and these are mixed in different proportions in different people. Diseases are often the result of disproportion in the mixture, and one needs to find out what that is. One also needs to know the influence of the stars, sun, moon and planets, for these affect both the potency of the herbs and the course of the disease as well as the nature of the patient. But there, I could go on all day.' I smiled and added, 'I still have much to learn. One can go on discovering more about this work, about herbs and diseases and the nature of people, all one's life, I think.'

'I would very much like to know more, Mr Judd. I mustn't keep you now'—for another customer was coming into the shop—'but I'll look in again, if I may. Thank you for your help.'

I had not given him any help that I knew of, apart from a little advice. But I did hope that he would be able to marry his Rachel one day, for they seemed so well suited for each other.

When I next went to the prison to visit Malachy the Keeper was as insolent as ever, and made me feel my efforts to be civil to him were fruitless.

'Ah, the friend of the he-witch!' he said. 'He's on his own now, so you can have him all to yourself. You had better get whatever spells you want from him now, for I doubt if he'll live till his trial.'

'You watch your tongue, man,' I said, for I found his attitude was making me angry. 'I have nothing to do with spells and witchcraft, and don't you forget it. As for Mr Moore, it's your responsibility to look after him. You have called me his friend—well, remember that, and take note that he's not friendless.'

'Pah!' was all he replied, as he led me down the passage.

The sight of Malachy saddened me, for I found a marked change for the worse in him. As the Keeper had said, he was on his own, the drunk and Robert Still both having gone, though something of their smell still seemed to hang in the air. Malachy sat hunched on the bench, sunk in a sort of lethargy from which he did not want to be roused. I reached down to touch his hand and asked how he was, but all he said was, 'Leave me be, zur.'

'Is there anything you want? Are you getting enough to eat?'

'Leave me be.'

And that was all I could get him to say, for he did not respond to anything else I said, and after trying for several minutes without success, I summoned the Keeper to let me out.

As we went along the passage to the street door I questioned the man more closely to see whether Malachy was getting proper food.

'Oh aye,' he assured me, 'he gets enough—more than an old he-witch deserves. But half the time he don't eat it. I've seen men like this before. Knowing they've nothing to live for, except death, they jus' fade away. I wouldn' be at all surprised if he didn' die before they get around to burnin' of him!'

I left feeling sad, but I was still at a loss as to what more I could do. When I thought about Mr Godwin's death I could see no way forward. If he had been murdered, the evidence was buried in Radipole churchyard, and I did not see how I could bring it home to either Sir James Freke or Mr Nathaniel Webb, supposing that either of them were guilty.

So I busied myself in my shop and about my work, and just hoped something new might turn up.

Then one Thursday morning a middle-aged man with a red weather-beaten face and a brown leather jerkin came into my shop and introduced himself as Richard Parker, Lady Alicia's groom.

'My lady is back,' he said, 'and has sent me to find you. She would like you to visit her at your earliest convenience to hear her news.'

'How did you do on your journey?' I asked.

'A rare time we had, with adventures on the way, and were nearly robbed, and then I myself became a thief on my lady's orders. But doubtless she will tell you all about it,' he replied. 'We had a bit of trouble to reach Lord Essex, but in the end we managed to find him, and ran him to earth somewhere beyond Wantage.'

'Where is the Earl now?'

'He's gone off west somewhere. I did hear that he was going to meet with General Waller. Certainly he was in a hurry to be gone, and my lady's visit seemed to throw him into a rare fit. I was waiting for her just outside the house where he was lodging, and he came out exclaiming, "Whatever shall I do?". And then he rode off muttering I know not what. But my lady will tell you all that happened, I'm sure.'

To me this did not sound very good news, but I was eager to hear all that she had to tell, good or bad, so I hurriedly walked after the groom to Wolfeton. This time the porter took me across the courtyard to the main house, where another manservant led me up a winding stone stair to a small wainscoted room where the Lady was sitting. There was an old tapestry on one wall and a cabinet against another, and two or three comfortable-looking chairs. A bow window faced towards the west.

She turned towards me as I entered and extended her hand for me to kiss. I was pleased to see a light in her eyes and a brightness in her manner that she had not had before her expedition.

'Mr Judd, I'm so relieved you came straight away,' she said, 'though I don't know that my news will be altogether pleasing to you.'

'I am most grateful to you for going, my lady,' I said, 'and at all events it's better to know the truth than to have false hopes, so I shall be glad to hear your news whatever it is.'

'Lord Essex has not given a definite yea or nay. But all is not yet lost, as you shall hear, so come and sit down, Mr Judd, and I will tell you all about it.'

So I sat in the comfortable armchair she indicated, and listened to her story.

Chapter 6 The Lady's adventures

I WILL TELL IT as it happened to us, (she said) for although you may think some of the details have little to do with the mission you entrusted to me I don't want to leave out anything that could be of importance. We have had such adventures, and some of the happenings on the way could affect the plans for the rising in Weymouth—you must judge.

We set off early before sunrise, and took the road to the north of Dorchester, so avoiding the town, and joined the London road a mile or so beyond the East Gate. I took with me my groom, Richard Parker, whom you've met, and Thomas Barnwell, a faithful retainer and old soldier, handy with his weapons in case of need.

We made good time to Puddletown and the next village—Milbourne, I think—though at the latter it was most unpleasant, for the children came out all in rags begging. They were very importunate and would not take no for an answer. The trouble was that if I had given to one I would have had to give to all, and had not enough for that. So we rode on, Thomas and Richard keeping the children away with their riding crops.

When they saw that we were not going to respond to their begging the children turned to cursing, and in this they were joined by their elders. We rode up the hill out of the village with their shouts and howls ringing in our ears. It was rather upsetting, and I never thought to see such insistent begging in England. But I suppose the war has made prices rise and the state of the poor more desperate. Certainly seeing and hearing them did more than anything else I have experienced to bring home to me the dreadful time poor people are having just now. But what can one do? Until these wars end they will continue to suffer.

At the top of the hill a lone traveller was waiting for us to catch up, a brown-clad man on a brown horse. His doublet, breeches and hat were all brown, and he had brown hair. He looked us up and down rather curiously. His manner was a bit over-bold, I thought, but he spoke quite politely.

'May I go along with you, lady?' he said, 'for there are long lonely stretches on this road, and it is not good to be a solitary traveller upon it. Indeed I have only just escaped from the villagers down there with my cloak still on my back!'

'Why certainly,' I said, for I could hardly say that I didn't like the look of him, and he spoke like a gentleman, though something about him made me slightly uneasy. And I was right, as I shall explain.

Anyway, we rode on together, and he told me he was a merchant of Winchester, who had been to see his old mother in Melcombe.

'Alas,' he said, 'I fear I have seen her for the last time. She is very old, near ninety, I believe, and infirm, poor soul, she can hardly take a step without help.'

He talked on about his mother in a way that would have brought tears to your eyes, but I wondered that he had not stayed at her bedside when (by his account) she was so at death's door. But he pleaded pressure of business as the reason for his leaving her, so I asked him about his work. He said he was a dealer in woollen cloth, who bought and sold all over the south of the country.

Now, as I think I told you, my home is in Hampshire and I know Winchester well, so I asked him his name and where exactly his business was. He said his name was Henry Smith, and that he had a warehouse down near the river.

There are men called Smith, of course, in fact there are too many, as you shall hear, but one does tend to be a little suspicious of a stranger who gives such a name. Also I could not recall seeing any wool-merchant's warehouse where he described. So I said, 'I have known Winchester all my life, and I can't remember seeing your warehouse.'

'Ah, lady,' he said with a smile, 'you could not have seen it, for

I have only just set up there, having moved from Hampton.' And so he went on, with a ready excuse for any discrepancies in his story.

Then he started asking me about my journey, where I was going and why. Because I did not entirely trust the man, I merely told him that I was a lady who had been staying with friends, and was now on my way to London. I said that I was travelling light because I had sent my baggage on ahead. I tried to make out that I had nothing of value with me in case he was thinking of trying to rob us.

Further to dissuade him from any evil he might be contemplating (though of course for all I knew he might be a perfectly innocent traveller) I asked him if he was skilful with sword or pistol, and when he said 'Not much', I told him of Thomas's prowess.

'My man has been a soldier,' I said, 'and fought in the Low Countries. You would not believe the number of men he has killed in his time, and he keeps in practice, I can tell you. With a man like that to guard us we shall be safe enough on this road.'

This perhaps displeased him, for when we were only about three miles from Blandford he made an excuse to leave us, saying his horse was going lame (although I had not noticed it) and he must find a smithy. He dismounted and waved us on, and I saw him still standing and gazing after us as we went over the next rise.

Thomas and Richard were also glad to leave him, for as Thomas said, 'There was something not quite above-board about that fellow.' Certainly I had found him a worry, because I did not believe his account of himself, and wondered what he wanted with us. I hoped now that he had given up thought of doing us harm, if that had been in his mind. But we had not seen the last of him, as you shall hear.

We stopped at an inn in Blandford to rest the horses and to take refreshment, and enquired if anyone was going on to Salisbury, for there is a very long and lonely stretch over the downs, and there would be safety in numbers.

There was another little party at the inn, two men and a woman, and the pot-boy told me they were about to leave on the Salisbury road, so I asked if we might go with them. They planned, they said, to get to Salisbury for the night, and would be glad of our company.

One of the men introduced himself as William Perry, the woman as his wife Juliana, and the other man simply as 'my friend'. He said they had been to a wedding in a nearby village—Charlton, I think he said—and were on their way home to near Winchester.

We rode on very happily together, for they were good company and kept us laughing. but when I said to the other man, 'I did not catch your name, sir,' he said, 'Henry'.

'Henry what?' I asked.

'Henry Smith.'

'But that is very odd,' I said, 'for between Dorchester and Blandford I met another man who said his name was Henry Smith. He came quite a long way with us.'

'My dear lady,' said the man, 'I am mortified and angry. I have been told that there is a man impersonating me, or at least taking my name. Tell me, was he dressed all in brown and on a brown horse?'

'He was,' I said, 'and claimed to be a wool-merchant of Winchester.'

'That's the very man,' he said. 'If I meet him I shall knock him down. What his game is I've no idea, but he can be up to no good, that's for certain.'

'But surely,' I said, 'there must be many men in England who are called Smith and who have been christened Henry. It could really be his name.'

'Could be, but I'll wager it isn't,' he said. 'Lady, I think you have had a lucky escape, for he might have robbed you.'

I confessed that such a thought had been in my own mind, and he assured me that with them I would be perfectly safe. So we rode on together until we were crossing those very lonely downs near where Dorset meets Hampshire and Wiltshire. A solitary traveller came cantering up from behind, and as he drew near I recognised him as the man in brown.

'Here comes your namesake,' I said, and was astonished when the second Henry Smith seized my reins and produced a pistol. At the same time the other man, William Perry (if that was his name) and the woman also produced pistols and ordered Thomas and Richard not to move.

The man in brown rode up and it was obvious that he knew our captors.

'You fool,' said the man holding me, 'why the devil did you tell this lady you were Henry Smith? You know that's the name I use, and you might have ruined everything.'

'There's no point in robbing her,' said the other. 'Her baggage has gone on ahead, she told me, so she won't have much about her.'

'She didn't tell me that,' said the first, 'and anyway she'll have some money and jewellery. So hand it over, lady,' he said to me, 'and you won't get hurt.'

'Our situation was looking unhappy, to say the least, but we were saved by a little troop of soldiers. I never thought to be glad to see Cavaliers, but in this case I was. They came trotting over a rise and distracted our captors. Thomas then drew his sword and wounded Perry, but was nearly hurt when the woman Juliana fired her pistol at him. Fortunately she missed, and when he lunged at her she turned her horse and galloped off.

At that the men also panicked and galloped after her, Perry having dropped his pistol and bleeding freely from where Thomas had cut his arm. The soldiers came up and asked what had happened, though the sight of the fleeing robbers and Thomas brandishing his sword must have made it fairly obvious. I thanked them heartily for their aid, and they congratulated Thomas on his quick action.

'I've been in many a fight in the wars overseas in days gone by,' he said, 'and there aren't many who could beat me at sword-play. But these wretches took us off guard.'

The captain of the troop asked me if I was all right. I had been feeling rather shaken, as you may imagine, but Thomas's calm acceptance of a fight like that as all in a day's work, shamed me into trying to show a brave front. So I laughed and said I felt the better for seeing him.

So he smiled and bowed, and he and his men went on their way, and we were soon trotting down the long hill to Coombe Bissett, and so to Salisbury. The streets there were very wet and mucky, in spite of the dry weather, because of the little streams that flow in the roadway. However, we found a good inn and I slept soundly, though Richard and Thomas were both much bitten by bugs in the night.

In the morning I asked the inn-keeper if he had any knowledge of Lord Essex's whereabouts, and he said it was thought that Essex was trying to prevent the King breaking out from Oxford. I therefore resolved to take the shortest way in that direction, going up the Bourne valley to Tidworth and aiming to go over the downs to cross the Thames at Hungerford.

Somehow, though, we missed a turning and went a little out of the way too far to the west, and found ourselves in a largish village. When we asked the people where we were they said it was Burbage, and that we were only three or four miles off our proper road. So we would not have been delayed much, except for the unlucky chance that we met another troop of Cavaliers.

We had stopped at the village inn for refreshment, when they came clattering into the yard. I was afraid they were going to commandeer our horses, and went out to confront them. Deciding that boldness was the best policy I raised my voice and said, 'Who the devil are you?'

'Captain Jenkins, at your service, ma'am,' said the officer, touching his helmet, 'and who may you be?'

I told him my name, and he then wanted to know where we were from and where going, and what our business was. He also demanded my pass, which of course I had not got. So I came all over the grand lady with him.

'My man,' I said, 'I expected better manners of those who serve the King. I am on my way to Oxford to pay my respects to His Majesty, and I shall certainly report to him how his soldiers are behaving.'

At that he looked somewhat abashed, and said:

'Pardon me, my lady, I did not know who you were, and one has to be alert for Roundhead messengers and spies.'

'Be easy, Captain,' I said, 'do I look like a Roundhead messenger or spy? Now, be a good fellow and direct me on the road to Hungerford, and tell me how to avoid the Earl of Essex and his troops, which I am told may be barring the way to Oxford.'

'Indeed, my lady, you had best go warily,' he said, 'for I believe he is around Wantage, which would be in your direct way. So you had better go further east than Hungerford, to Newbury at least, before you go north, and thus give Wantage a wide berth.'

I thanked him, and would have ridden to Hungerford and from there straight to find the Earl, but Captain Jenkins was so eager for me to give a good report of him to the King that he insisted on escorting me to Newbury, which took us seven or eight miles beyond our shortest road.

However, there I persuaded him to leave me at an inn, for I said I was tired and needed to rest. But as soon as he had gone well away I roused Thomas and Richard, and we set off, crossing the river at Newbury and heading straight for Wantage, where we arrived in the late afternoon. There I saw more soldiers, and was glad to find that they were from Lord Essex's troops. From them I learnt that he was a mile or two up the road, and so eventually I tracked him down in a village where he was lodging at the parsonage.

He was most surprised to see me.

'My dear Alicia,' he said, 'what! are you alone? not with your father? Whatever has possessed you to come into danger like this?'

He went on to tell me that patrols of Cavaliers from Oxford were ranging all about, and that if I met with any such I might suffer insult or worse.

'And even my soldiers do not always behave as they should,' he added, 'so you ought really to have more protection than a couple of servants.'

I told him about our encounter with Captain Jenkins and his patrol, and made him laugh at my coming over all the grand lady with them. However, I wasted no more time, and gave him your letter from the Weymouth people. He read it with a frown, so I feared he was disliking what it proposed. But then he exclaimed:

'By God, Alicia, there is nothing I would like more than to abandon this wretched cat-and-mouse watching for the King, waiting for him to leave the safety of Oxford, and instead to sweep through Dorset and the west country. But what can I do? Parliament wants me to stay here, or follow the King if he breaks out. But what this letter says is absolutely right, for if he brings in more of the French we'll have the devil to pay.'

He then asked me how I came by the letter, and how far what it promised could be trusted. I told him I had been given it to bring to him by a very worthy man (that's you, Mr Judd) who had brought it from the conspirators in Weymouth.

'Think,' I said, 'dear Uncle Robert, they are offering you a triumph which could be the turning-point in this war. And after taking hold of Melcombe and Weymouth you will then go on to relieve Lyme and clear the whole west country of Cavaliers.'

'You're right, Alicia, by heaven you are. And I would like to,' he said, 'by God I would like to. Believe me, Alicia, when I say that I'm tired to death of hanging about here waiting for the King to make a move. Nothing would please me more than to make a foray into Dorset and capture Weymouth, and perhaps go further west and, as you say, raise the siege of Lyme and send that young brute Prince Maurice to hell with a flea in his ear. But Parliament are very insistent that I stay here.'

'Then is nothing to be done?' I said. 'Are the French to be allowed free entry into England, and perhaps change the whole course of this war?'

'Certainly someone ought to prevent them,' he agreed. 'I

suppose Waller could go.'

'That would not do,' I told him. 'You are the man needed in Dorset, and he is not. The Weymouth people insist that it must be you or no one. They will only rise if they have someone come that they can trust. So, dear Uncle Robert, it must be you.'

'I'll tell you what I will do,' he said. 'I'll ride over to see Waller, and will decide with him what to do. If I can leave him watching the King, I might defy Parliament and do what you ask.'

As it was late I spent the night nearby in a poor sort of inn, where the beds were dirty and uncomfortable and the food poor.

In the morning I waited on Lord Robert again and found he was still very undecided. In fact he was worried and agitated.

'Whatever shall I do?' he said. 'If I obey Parliament I shall stay here watching the King, and then the French may indeed land and change things for the worse. It must surely be in the south that defeat or victory will come. So I have a mind to defy Parliament. Too many of them are pot-house generals, who wouldn't know one end of a pike from the other. But they will be exceedingly angry if I disobey them. It would be much simpler to do nothing, and stay here as they want. But doing nothing doesn't gain victories! Well, Alicia, I'm off to meet Waller at Stow-on-the-Wold, and I really don't know which way to jump.'

'May I leave my man Thomas Barnwell with you?' I said. 'If he may ride with you to Stow, whatever you resolve, he can bring the news to us by the shortest way. If you do decide to come we must let our people in Weymouth know, so that they can be ready.'

He agreed to that, so I have left Thomas there with orders to ride back here as fast as he can when he has heard definitely what Lord Essex decides to do. Essex rode off with Thomas and a small escort, and I and Richard rode back home.

But I must tell you one more thing. You will be wondering why I have been telling you about my journey with so many particulars, but the most extraordinary thing happened on our way back. We had got to Salisbury without mishap, and put up there at the same inn as before. After I had had my supper Richard came to me and said there was someone I knew in the bar.

'What do you mean?' I asked him.

'That man in brown who tried to rob us —he's down there drinking strong ale. Do you think we ought to confront him, my lady, or denounce him to a magistrate?'

'No, Richard,' I said, after thinking it over, 'it would simply be our word against his, and we could prove nothing, and it would delay us when we need to get home as quickly as we can. But we want avoid falling in with him on the road tomorrow, so you go back to the bar and see if you can overhear his plans. If he recognises you, no matter, for it may well make him nervous and cause him to go away.'

So off Richard went, and later that evening he came and knocked on my door.

'My lady,' he said, 'that man—he's wormed his way into the confidence of a merchant and his wife. He has been telling them all about his old mother in Winchester, and how he has had to leave her almost at the point of death. Last time she was in Melcombe, wasn't she? Anyway he has arranged to go along with this couple to Blandford tomorrow.'

'And rob them on the way, no doubt,' I said. 'How can we prevent him? We had better warn them.'

'If we could somehow stop him from leaving...' said Richard.

'I know,' I said, for I had an idea, 'when he's sound asleep you must steal his clothes. He can hardly travel naked.'

'But I can't do that, my lady,' Richard protested, 'supposing he wakes up?' But I wouldn't listen to his objections.

'If he wakes and catches you I shall take the blame,' I said, 'and I shall tell everyone how he threatened us with a pistol and would have robbed us. But don't wake him, and all will be well.'

'But what shall I do with his clothes?'

'Bring them to me,' I said. 'Don't worry how late it may be—bring them straight here.'

Fortunately, though, the man went to bed quite early, having drunk rather more than he ought, I suspect, and was soon snoring like a pig, Richard told me. He came to my door with an armful of clothes—britches, doublet, drawers, stockings and even boots. All that was lacking was his shirt, which the fellow was sleeping in.

Richard said there were papers in a pocket, so when he had gone off to his bed I had them out and saw that there were a couple of letters and a paper containing a long list of names. Two things caught my eye: one of the letters was from Sir James Freke, and at the head of the list was the name of Nathaniel Webb, and I remembered that you had mentioned Mr Webb was leader of our people in Weymouth and that Sir James Freke was a danger to them.

That was yesterday morning. We reached home safely last night, and this morning I sent Richard to fetch you.

Lady Alicia had come to the end of her narrative, and sat gazing at me with her hands clasped under her chin.

'What do you think it all means, Mr Judd?' she said at last.

'Have you got these papers?' I asked.

'Indeed I have. I thought this Mr Smith—or is he Mr Sutler? for that's the name one of the letters is addressed to—deserved any inconvenience or loss we could inflict upon him, if we were unable to get him hanged. So I stuffed his clothes and boots up the chimney and have brought the papers here.'

She opened a drawer and took out two letters and the list of names. There were about thirty names on the list, and I saw that besides Nathaniel Webb there were George Godwin and Obadiah Horner. Undoubtedly this was a list of the chief Roundhead conspirators in Melcombe and Weymouth.

One of the letters, as Lady Alicia had said, began 'Dear Mr Sutler', and was brief but significant. In it Sir James thanked Mr Sutler for his 'valuable services' and hoped that the enclosure would encourage him to 'render further assistance'. So presumably he had been paid for information given. The other letter was from a woman, and began 'Dearest Harry' and ended 'Your loving Bunny'. Perhaps his name really was Henry.

How much had Henry Smith or Sutler told Sir James to pass on to the Royalist Governor? Did the presence of the list in the man's pocket mean that he had not yet given the names to Sir James? Or was it a copy of what he had told Sir James? Or maybe he had told Sir James some of the names, but was feeding the information in small amounts in order to gain more money.

At all events Mr Webb must be told, in order for him and the others to be on their guard, and I just hoped that whatever Mr Sutler had passed on would not be enough to foil their plans. Further light was also cast upon George Godwin. The fact that he was on the list, and that information was probably getting to Sir James not from Godwin but from Henry Sutler, suggested that Godwin had not been a double agent.

Yet this made little difference to the problem of who might have killed him, because if Mr Webb had thought he had betrayed them Webb might have killed him even though he was innocent. And Sir James might have killed him to try to foil the Roundhead's plot.

I thanked Lady Alicia for all she had accomplished, and her face lit up with pleasure.

'I've never had so much fun in my life,' she said. 'The sight of that man, Smith or Sutler or whatever his name is, wrapped in his shirt and a blanket and shouting at the innkeeper that his clothes had been stolen—I shall never forget it! We rode to Blandford with the merchant and his wife, and told them what an escape they had had, and I laughed and they laughed and Richard laughed—oh, my sides still ache with laughing!'

'How do you think Lord Essex will decide?' I asked.

'I wish I could tell,' she said. 'He had not made up his mind when we parted, and I fear he lacks that spark of—what should one say?—of the gambler, willing to risk all on one throw. But I suppose prudence is a virtue in a general. However, all is not lost yet, though things are in the balance. He is sorely tempted to come,

I am sure, but his fears of what may happen if he disobeys Parliament may dissuade him. I think the danger of the French coming (which I stressed) weighed most heavily with him. But whether that will be enough to persuade him to come I have no idea.'

'Did he write any reply to the Weymouth people's letter?'

'No, he decided he would leave it until after his meeting with Waller. I asked him what reply I should bring back, and he said, "Tell them that I am considering their proposal", and he added, "Oh, and thank them heartily".'

'So the only message I can pass on is that he is considering?'

'I'm afraid so. What do you think the Weymouth people will do?'

'They will be disappointed, not a doubt of that. But I suppose Essex may yet decide to come here for, whatever Parliament says, it would surely make sense to deny the Cavaliers use of the port.'

'I am so angry,' she said. 'It's so obvious what needs doing, but he won't make up his mind to do it. He dithers. That's why he didn't do better at Edgehill fight. Oh, if only I were a man!'

'You have done great service, my lady,' I said. 'I will send your news to the people at Melcombe without delay, and tell them that we have to await Lord Essex's decision.'

'And you will tell me if there is anything else I can do, more messages to take or people to see? I feel so much better for having done something. You have no idea what a wonderful cure for melancholy that is!'

'I am very glad, my lady,' I said, 'and be assured that if I find there is more that you can do I will come to you at once.'

After I left her I walked round to the stables to see how the boy Robin was doing, and was pleased to find that his hand was healing well and that he was back at work with the horses. So after warning him to take care of himself, I walked back through the meadows the direct way to Dorchester.

As I went I considered the situation. There was not much to tell the plotters, but they must be prepared to take action quickly if Essex did decide to come, for he could be here within a week or so if he moved fast, and so they ought to be informed. But today being Thursday it would be five days before I could send a message by the tranter. I did not want to go myself, for I had too much work to attend to. How was I to pass the news to them?

Chapter 7 Malachy's angel

THEN I BETHOUGHT ME of Jacob Perrin. He was the small farmer and smuggler whose cart I had recovered a few months ago after it had been stolen by soldiers and was in fact my friend Lawrence Huatt's brother-in-law (though Lawrence was rather ashamed of the connection). Jacob had amply repaid me, and had found a good horse for me to buy, but I knew he often went on journeys to the coast, journeys best not inquired about too closely, and I was sure he would not mind carrying a package for me.

So when I reached home I wrote a letter as follows:

Sir,

Your letter was delivered, but the doctor is undecided whether to recommend sea air or retiring into the country, and has gone to consult with his fellow-physician. As soon as I hear his decision I will let you know. Meanwhile keep the patient warm and exercised. But take special care, for I have heard of a dangerous infection carried by a certain Henry Sutler that has spread to Upwey and which could be fatal.

M.Judd, Apothecary.

I wrapped it round a box of pills and addressed the package to Mr Webb, and that evening rode out to Monkton, the little village a couple of miles south of the town. When I reached Jacob Perrin's tumbledown farm I was glad to find him at home. He was in the barn digging a hole in the floor, and had reached a depth of four feet or so. His mongrel dog came running out at me barking furiously but wagging its tail, and Perrin scrambled out of the hole and shook my hand.

'Why Micah,' he said, 'I was jus' thinken o' you, an' laughing to meself at the way you got back me cart.'

'What are you doing here?' I asked.

'Ah, this is going to be another hidey-hole. If the so'jers or the coast Watchers (supposing we get those pests back again) come looking for me stuff, I want to give 'em summat to find. They'll come bangin' an' thumpin' all about, as they do, an' they'll hear a hollow-sounding place here, an' get all rafted an' raptured about it, an' they'll dig it up an' find it empty. "Oh yes," I'll say (for there's no point in denying what I've done in the past—they know it), "at one time you might a' found things there that ought not to be. But I'm reformed," I'll tell 'em, "I'm a good Puritan or Catholic", or whatever it's best to be at the time—Church of England I expect is safest, if one's not sure—"an' you won't find me doing wrong now." An' they'll say, "Bless you, brother," an' go away without further ado. Good idea, eh?'

'You are an old rogue, Mr Perrin, and I'm ashamed to be associated with you,' I said, slapping him on the back.

'Ah, 'tis people like you, and my good brother-in-law in Dorchester, who keep me respectable. But what brings you here, Micah, for I don't think you'ld come all this way of an evenin' jus' to see me.'

'Jacob, I always like to see you. Every time I mount this horse I think of you. But you're right, I have a favour to ask, if it won't put you to too much trouble. Will you be going to Melcombe in the next day or two?'

'Well now, a worthy man like you wouldn't want to know where I'm likely to go, now would ye? However, let's say I could go to Melcombe. There's no crime it that. I could go tomorrow if you wanted. Also there's a sea-captain I want to have a word with, an' I guess I'll find him in the Ship Inn by the quay. So yes, what can I do for you?'

'It's to deliver this package of pills.' I explained how to find Mr Webb's house. 'It's important it gets to this man to keep the patient alive.'

He gave me a shrewd look, and I'm sure he guessed that there was more at stake than a patient's health. He probably realised that I did not have patients who lived in Melcombe. But he did not ask questions, simply saying:

'Have no fear, it shall be delivered.'

We walked over to his cottage for him to put the package away safely until he could take it on the morrow. His house was untidy and somewhat cheerless, for he lived alone. He had a woman who came in once a week to do his washing and a little cleaning, but I had the impression that she was a bit of a slut and didn't do as much as she ought.

He saw me glance around and seemed to feel my disapproval for he said:

'Miriam comes tomorrow to clean up; not that she does much.'

'You really need a woman to live in, Jacob,' I said. 'If you don't want to marry again, a housekeeper would soon have the place in order.'

'I had enough o' being kept in order when my wife Joan was alive,' he said. 'She was a good woman, kept the place well enough, an' I was sorry when she died. But I wasn't sorry to be on me own again. Now if I had an odd job man about the place I could do wi' that. I'm often away, as you know,'—He gave me a wink—'an' someone to keep an eye on the place would be useful.'

He went to a room beyond the kitchen and came back with a couple of tankards of ale, and we sat and talked. He wanted to find out what I might have heard about movements of armies, so that he could avoid them if they were coming to the south country again.

"I'm not so worried about the Cavaliers in Weymouth,' he said, 'for they seem to be content to stay in the town and don't trouble the country round about. But Poole and Wareham are different. Those Sydenham brothers, they stir up trouble. Oh, I know they may be excellent soldiers and very valuable to the Parliament. But they will keep comin' out wi' their raidin' parties, and if I happened to be in their way I'd lose me horse and cart again, and its contents, and'd be lucky to escape wi' me life. An' then there's the Cavaliers in Wareham now, breathin' fire and sword to all comers, and ransackin' all over the place, God rot 'em!'

'I know—and who can tell where they may turn up next?' I agreed. 'You'll just have to keep your eyes and ears open, Jacob. But I should warn you of another lot of soldiers who may come this way. Don't breathe a word of it to anyone else though, and it's not certain that they're coming. But if they comes they'll pass through Dorchester, I've no doubt.'

As soon as the words were out of my mouth I regretted them, for I feared it was unwise even to give him a hint as vague as that. Yet there was really little danger of alerting the garrison in Weymouth, for they must be aware that they would be a likely target if a Roundhead army entered Dorset again. Also Perrin was a discreet fellow, as with his line of business he needed to be, and would not spread rumours.

So we went on to discuss the war, and the resulting hardships folk were suffering, and the divided state of Dorchester. At last I rose and said farewell, and rode quietly home in the dusk.

It was soon after this that I saw Matthew Barton again. He came to my shop and asked more questions about my work. He showed so much interest that I let him try pounding some seeds in the mortar and measuring out ointment into small bottles for sale. I was pleased to see that he was careful and exact and, except when he was talking about his difficulties with his father over Rachel, was a cheerful and pleasant young man.

But my worries about possible uprisings and about Malachy must have shown in my face, for after a time Matthew remarked:

'You look sad today, Mr Judd. Is anything wrong?'

I could not tell him about the plots, but there could be no harm in sharing my concerns about Malachy.

'Yes,' I said, 'I've been visiting an old fellow in the prison. You may have heard of him, for there was clamour enough when he was brought in. He's likely to be condemned as a witch and for a murder. I think the murder was done by someone else, but I can't prove it. And another difficulty is, the old man thinks his curses really did cause the death, so he's likely to plead guilty, or at least not defend himself at all. And now he's sinking into deep melancholy.'

I explained how Malachy came to be in prison, and his own belief in the power of his cursing, but added firmly that I did not think he had such powers or had any connections with the Evil One. I described the sad state he was now in, and how I had been unable to rouse him.

'I didn't see him brought to prison,' said Matthew, 'but father mentioned him the other day. Father believes he's an evil wizard or he-witch and has satanic powers. Don't you believe witchcraft is dangerous, Mr Judd?'

'Witchcraft may be, but I'm sure old Malachy isn't. He's just a poor deluded old man whose neighbours feared him perhaps. He has some strange gifts, but I don't believe they're from the devil.'

I told Matthew about Malachy's skill with the hazel-rod, and the way he used to talk to his cat as if it was a person.

'But I've met other lonely old people who talk to their pets,' I said. 'It doesn't mean that the cat or dog, or even the chicken I once saw an old woman keeping inside her cottage as a pet, is possessed by Satan. As for the dangers of witchcraft, I don't really know what to think. Witches come in the Bible, of course, and we're told not to have anything to do with them and their practices. But I think a Christian's spiritual armour ought to be protection enough against anything the Evil One can do. So although I meet some very odd folk in the course of my work, and some evil ones, I've never had real cause to fear the devil. I admit I was a bit afraid when Malachy was first brought to prison, but he's now in such a sad and dreadful state that no sane person could fear him,'

'But if other people think he's a witch they'll be afraid?'

'Yes, and the trouble is their fear will make them eager to get rid of him, to kill him, as his neighbours in Upwey would have done. I suppose I do run a risk if I try to help him, not from any harm he would do me, but if people started to shun me for seeing him, and so didn't come to my shop or want my services any more. But that's a risk I'll have to take.'

I thought no more about this conversation at the time, for Matthew asked no more about him and left soon after, and for the next couple of days I was very busy. Also I was worried about Agnes, whose time to give birth was approaching in a few weeks, and although she seemed in good health, I had seen too many young wives die in childbirth not to fear that I might lose her.

However, on next Lord's Day I did go to see Malachy again, without much hope that I would be any more successful in rousing him from his sad state than I had been before, but more from a sense of duty. So I was surprised to find him sitting up and looking more like his old self. He was clean, his hair had been trimmed and tidied, and there was the old gleam in his eye.

'What has happened to you?' I asked.

'What do you mean, zur?'

'You look better, you've had a wash...'

'Ah, zur, I be havin' a visitation by an angel.'

Had his mind finally given way? I wondered.

'What do you mean?'

''Tis an angel from heaven, zur. She came to me yesterday. I told her to let me be, but she wouldn' listen. She scrubbed me clean, an' put on me a clean shirt, an' did this an' that, so's I hardly know myself.'

'And who was she?'

'That I don' know, zur. I axed her, "You be an angel," I said, "where be you from?" an' she jus' laughed an' went away. But she said she'd come back.'

'It was a woman then, not a real angel?'

'No zur, I tell 'ee, she were an angel straight from heaven. Why she should come to an ol' sinner like me, I don' know, when me curses ha' sent a man to his death, though he deserved it. But come to me she did, an' I bless her for it.'

And that was all I could find out from him. Even the gaol-keeper, as he let me out, was no more informative.

'Old Malachy says he's been visited by an angel,' I said. 'What does he mean?'

'Arrh,' he said, 'he could be right an' all.'

The mystery as to who the 'angel' might be was solved when Matthew came into my shop again. He asked more questions about the various herbs and how I prepared them in medicines and ointments. I told him how I make distilled waters of plants, and the difference between syrups and juleps, and mentioned decoctions, electuaries, conserves and lohocks (which, in case you don't know, are like syrups, only thicker). I thought by showing off a little I might satisfy him and he would lose interest, but instead I seemed to excite him more.

'Syrups preserve the virtue of flowers or herbs,' I told him. 'When you have steeped the water well with the plants you add sugar or honey, which will preserve their goodness for a year or more. There are three different sorts of syrups: infused, decocted, or made with juice. I'll show you sometime, if you care to come and see me at work. Juleps, on the other hand, don't keep, and one makes them up for immediate use. They are pleasant drinks, very good for invalids, and may be made sweet or bitter or a mixture of both.'

'What are decoction and electuaries?' he wanted to know. 'I hope you don't mind me asking you, Mr Judd, but I find all this very interesting.'

'It seems to me that you will want to become an apothecary yourself,' I said.

'I have thought of it, Mr Judd, but I suppose my father will want me to follow his trade and become a mercer.'

'To be an apothecary you need really to like seeing people who are sick, and not be afraid of diseases,' I remarked. 'But I must say that one of my greatest joys is to see someone who has been ill restored to health after taking my preparations. As for the difference between various ways of preparing medicines, decoctions, electuaries and so on—really the best way would be to show you. So if you truly want to learn more you had better come and watch me at work.'

'Thank you, sir,' he said, 'I should very much like to do that.'

He then asked me how 'the old man in prison' was doing.

'It is extraordinary the change in him,' I replied. 'I found him clean and cheerful (as far as anyone could be in that prison awaiting trial and possible death), and convinced that he had been visited by an angel!'

'I think I know who the angel is,' said Matthew. 'I hope you don't mind, sir, but I told Rachel about the old man, and how you thought he was unjustly accused, and what a sad state he was in, and she said she would do something about it. She's very determined once she has an idea, Mr Judd, and nothing I could say could dissuade her.'

'Bless her!' I said. 'She really has been a ministering angel to old Malachy.'

'Have you found out anything that could prove his innocence, sir?'

'I'm afraid not. I just don't know what to do. But I hope, if he does come to trial, he may be persuaded to plead not guilty, and that the judge or justice is a man of sympathy. Unfortunately old Malachy is still convinced that it was his curse that caused the death of the other man, so do tell your Rachel to try to get that out of his head.'

'How is that, sir? Why does the old man think his curse was so powerful?'

'Between you and me, Matthew, I think his Rector in Upwey has a lot to answer for. He has excommunicated Malachy in effect, and made him feel that he's a damned soul. So when Malachy cursed this Mr George Godwin who was wronging him, and Mr Godwin fell dead shortly afterwards, it seemed that the curse had had the power of the Evil One. Not only the neighbours thought that, but Malachy himself—and I can't get him to think otherwise.'

'But do you know what really killed this Mr Godwin?'

'No, but I know he had enemies, and more than one person who had a motive to kill him. I can't tell you all the details, but it has to do with Roundheads and Cavaliers and various plots. Has your father talked to you about any of these things?'

I wondered whether Matthew knew the part his father was playing in the plans to overthrow the Cavaliers in Dorchester. But in any case I did not feel I ought to tell him any details of what was going forward in Melcombe and Weymouth.

'No,' he said, 'father doesn't discuss things with me. He often speaks harshly of Cavaliers, and I sometimes wonder if he's plotting anything, but I don't expect he'd tell me if he were.'

'I expect he would want to keep you out of danger. But thinking again of Malachy, if Rachel could try to persuade him that he is not responsible for Godwin's death she would be doing him great service.'

'I will ask her,' he promised.

'Thank you, Matthew. She has already been a blessing to him. I only hope she will be more successful than I have been in getting him to resist his enemies!'

He went out smiling. Our next meeting would not be so happy.

Chapter 8 An unexpected hitch

ON THE NEXT MONDAY afternoon as I returned from seeing a man with sore eyes I found Richard Parker, Lady Alicia's groom, waiting outside my door.

'Lady Alicia's compliments, sir, and would you please come to her. She asked me to say that she has some good news to impart.'

'I shall come right away,' I said, 'as soon as I have told my wife where I'm going. You go on ahead, and tell the Lady I am on my way.'

I then had a word with Agnes, and said I would see her for supper, took my best cloak, and set off to walk to Wolfeton.

This time I was shown into the handsome old hall. The wainscotted walls were somewhat dark, but over the fireplace were a line of striking carved figures—fourteen kings of England, including our present King Charles. I remembered being told that just before the outbreak of the present troubles the sceptre fell from his hand, a most ill omen, but I saw that it had been replaced. Other figures, an abbot, a horseman and soldiers, were opposite, and a stone staircase led up at the far end.

But I had no time to observe more for, stepping off the stairs as I entered, was Lady Alicia.

After greeting me she told me the news without further ado.

'My man Thomas, whom I left with Lord Essex, as I told you, arrived back this afternoon. He has great news—Lord Essex is on his way, and will move his army to Weymouth as soon as may be.'

'Great news indeed!' I said. 'When do you think he will arrive?'

'Uncle Robert is sometimes too much like a snail,' she said, 'but he can move fast when his mind is clearly made up. And it seems to have become clear at last. Apparently he said he was prepared to disobey Parliament for the greater good of the Cause, for he sees the importance of securing Weymouth—and indeed of driving Prince Maurice away from Lyme, to deny the King all access to this coast.'

'Today is Monday,' I said. 'Do you think he could be here within a week?'

'Why not?' she said. 'Armies do seem to lumber along very slowly, but he could send his cavalry on ahead, and they could be here in three or four days or even less.'

'He will need his foot soldiers and big guns if he is to capture the castles—unless of course our people manage to surprise the garrisons, as the Cavaliers did at Portland last year.'

'I suppose the horsemen could take the towns, and the castles could be left until the main body of the army catches up?'

'That is true,' I agreed, 'so in case he does send cavalry on ahead I had better go back at once and alert our people both in Dorchester and Weymouth.'

I thanked her for her information and her foresight in leaving Thomas behind to bring the news, and hurried away.

I was walking rapidly across the meadows and had reached the road to Dorchester, when a couple of horsemen came riding up behind me.

'Here's another—he'll do,' said one loudly and, 'Stand, you! You're our prisoner.'

'Who the devil are you?' I said, 'and what tyranny is this, to stop a man on the highroad like this?'

I saw that they were soldiers, though I did not know from which side, as arms and armour were much alike for both.

'Be easy man,' he said, 'we're not going to hurt you. You are now a soldier of the King.'

'But this is nonsense,' I said. 'I am a citizen and shopkeeper of Dorchester, a man of property. You can't impress me like this.'

'We can and we have,' he said. 'The King needs men, and you're a man, I trust, so you'll do.'

'I protest,' I said, 'this is an outrage.'

'You talk too much,' he said. 'You'll do to fill out a rank as much as any man. Bring 'im along.'

I saw that the man in charge was a sergeant, and at his command the other rider dismounted and tied a rope round my neck. It was useless to resist men armed with swords and pistols, so I kept quiet, resolving to escape as soon as the opportunity occurred. Some more soldiers arrived, led by a Captain, and I saw that they had several prisoners roped as I was.

The soldier tied the other end of my rope to another prisoner, then remounted, and in this ignominious fashion tied together like slaves we were led along towards Dorchester. Where the road crosses the River Frome we waited, and presently another party of soldiers came down from the direction of the town with more prisoners. There must have been about forty of us conscripted men, most (I guessed from their clothes) from the poorer parts of the town, but there were one or two tradesmen or shopkeepers like myself, and to my surprise I saw that Matthew Barton was also amongst them. We greeted one another with a look, but could not speak for the sergeant was shouting, 'No talking there! Silence for Captain Treves.'

The Captain cast his eye over the bedraggled-looking party, and then addressed us:

'Now you men, Lord Hopton needs reinforcements, and it is the duty of every able-bodied man to fight for the King, so you have been chosen to join his forces and fight the rebels. You may be sad or angry at this moment because you have been picked; but before long we'll make soldiers of ye, and if ye have any sense of honour ye'll be proud to be serving His Majesty. Obey orders, knuckle down to your duties, and all will be well. Try to desert, and you will be hanged. God save the King!—Right, carry on, sergeant.'

He rode to the head of the party and, with mounted soldiers all around us, we set off in a disorderly bunch—I can hardly say we marched—back up the Sherborne road. They jostled us through the village of Charminster and along the valley going north, and in spite of the sergeant's efforts to make us keep in step we continued to shuffle along raggedly.

'Come along there. Keep in step. Keep moving,' he kept shouting. 'Keep up—we've got to get to Sherborne. Move your bloody feet!'

As if in response, a middle-aged man near the front stumbled and fell to his knees.

'Get up!' roared the sergeant.

'Get up!' shouted the nearest soldier, leaning from his horse to swipe at the man with a long stick he was carrying. 'Come on, off your knees, you laggard. You'll have time to pray later—and more to pray about!'

The prisoners beside the fallen man helped him to his feet and we went on. But that was only one of a number of similar incidents, and it was soon clear to me that we wouldn't reach Sherborne that night.

As we walked my thoughts were mostly of how I could escape, though I was also worried about Agnes. She would not know what had happened to me, though she would surely hear that men had been conscripted to fight for the King, and might guess that I was amongst them. But not knowing for certain would be most distressing for her, and the heartlessness of the conscription appalled me. I have never felt so against the King and his supporters as I did then, not even when Prince Maurice's soldiers were ravaging Dorchester the year before.

As for escape, I could not believe that I could be forced to join the King's, or Lord Hopton's, army. These soldiers would surely find it impossible to hold us all, and if any escaped I was determined I would be among them. Meanwhile all we could do was to go as slowly as they would let us, and to take as long as possible to get to Sherborne.

We had been going along the valley road, and paused for a rest in the village of Godmanstone. The sergeant allowed us to sit at the road-side for a few minutes, and to share a jug of water which was passed around. I was able to exchange a few words with Matthew.

'How did you come to be picked up?' I asked.

'I was just walking up the High Street,' he said. 'The soldiers were rounding up anyone they could catch, and I didn't get out of their way quick enough.'

'We'll have to go along with them for the moment, Matthew, but tonight we must do our best to escape.'

Meanwhile the sergeant was conferring with the officer, who had been showing signs of impatience at our slow progress, and who had evidently come to the conclusion that long before we got to Sherborne we would have to halt for the night. He gave the sergeant an order, and rode away ahead of us and disappeared round a bend.

The sergeant shouted to us to stand, which we did rather stiffly.

'Now you men,' he said, 'you're so slow we'll never get you to Sherborne by nightfall. So we'll make for Cerne and spend the night there. It's only another two or three miles, I believe, and if you behave yourselves you'll have a bite to eat and some hay to sleep on. We'll make soldiers of you yet.'

So on we went. Now that the Captain had gone, and with the prospect of soon halting for the night, the soldiers seemed more friendly and relaxed, though they kept a firm eye on us to see that no one tried to escape. I even managed to engage the soldier nearest to me in conversation.

'Have you been in the army long?' I asked.

'Yea, long enow,' he said. 'I coome from Lord Hopton's lands in Zomerset,'—His speech was certainly from that part—'and ha' been wi' him since the start, when he first went to Sherborne.'

'Have you seen much fighting?'

'Aye, a fair amount. Lord Hopton led us down into Cornwall, and we beat the Roundheads at Braddock Down. That was easy, 'cause we won. But Lansdown, now that were a horrid bloody fight. Lord Hopton himself was shot in the arm, and then near killed when the powder waggon blew up. Aye, I wouldn'a want to be in many fights like Lansdown.'

'What have you been doing in Dorset?' I asked.

'Not zo mouch o' late, not that I care. We've just been down to the sea-coast with supplies of ammunition for the garrison at Weymouth. Easy place they have there—plenty o' food, plenty o' young maidens, and no fighting.'

'Yet I suppose they have to be ready to fight, to defend themselves against Roundhead raids or plots.'

''Ees,' he agreed, 'but down to Weymouth they be well out o' the way, and they'ld have plenty o' warning if the Roundheads were approaching. As for plots, if any of the townspeople tried to rebel they would be put down soon enough. In fact while we were there our lads in the garrison were saying they had just foiled some plot.'

'How was that?'

'Oh, a local gen'leman, Sir James somebody, got wind o' some crack-brained scheme to overpower the garrison. Apparently he discovered that one of his relations was involved with the plotters and so Sir James was able to tell the Governor all about it.'

'What happened to Sir James's relation?'

'The plotter?—I did hear he'd been killed, but I don't know how or where. If he really revealed everything to Sir James he deserved a reward. But at anyrate the plot was foiled.'

I considered this as we passed the turning to Nether Cerne and began the last mile and a half to Cerne Abbas. What the soldier said seemed to confirm that Godwin's death was not from natural causes, but whether he had been killed by his cousin or by his fellow plotters I still could not decide. At all events, I was sure that Malachy could not be the murderer. But whatever I thought would not help him, even if I were able to escape and testify at his trial, unless I could find out the truth. If the murder could not be brought home to the real culprit the accusation of witchcraft would be very difficult to refute.

The talk of plotters in Weymouth reminded me that if their plans were to be put into effect they needed to know that the Earl of Essex was coming, so that they could rise at the right moment. But how could I tell them, prisoner as I was? Even if Lady Alicia heard that I had been conscripted (which she probably would not), she would not know who to pass the news to. Mr Barton, too, who was no doubt very anxious about his son, ought to be informed, so that Dorchester might be in readiness. But here was I, the only person knowing all the people who should be told, helpless.

At last we entered the outskirts of Cerne, but instead of turning right into the village we turned left a short way and stopped at a farm. We were herded into a barn, and the doors shut and barred. There was some hay stacked at one end and a rough earth floor. Light came in through tall slits, too narrow for a body to squeeze through.

We untied each other's bonds and conferred in low tones. I went over to Matthew and asked him how he was.

'A bit footsore,' he answered, 'but sorer of heart. I'm wondering what my parents are thinking. We were taken off the street, and not given the chance even say good-bye to our families.'

'I know,' I said, 'they took me as I was walking home on the highway, and my poor wife will be terribly worried. So we've got to escape. We really must break out somehow. Let's have a look around and see if there's any way of getting out of this place.'

We went round together to look at the doors. The barn was the usual shape, with two long ends and a threshing-floor in the centre, with high double doors at each side. We peeped through cracks and saw that there were sentries on both sides. When we tried the doors they would not open. Heavy bars of wood had been fixed outside, and when we rattled the door a sentry shouted, 'Get away from there, you dam' idle dogs!'

We looked at the slit windows, but they had solid cut stone surrounds as did the doors. The rest of the wall was plastered and had once been whitewashed, though now streaked with mud and dirt. In places the plaster had broken away showing that the walls were made of chalky rubble, no doubt built like cob. This is a common way of building in our part of the country. Clay or chalk is wetted and put between wooden shuttering, stamped down hard and left to dry before the shuttering is moved up a stage and the next layer of wall added. Provided the rain is kept out with plaster and a good roof such a wall will last for centuries, but it is softer than stone and may be dug away with a pick.

We did not have a pick, and I and Matthew looked all around for something to use as a tool. We found in a corner, half hidden by a pile of old hay, an iron rod about four feet long, with a point at one end and a ring through a hole at the other, evidently a post for driving into the ground to tether an animal.

'Do you think we could dig our way out?' asked Matthew.

'We'll try,' I said, 'but I'm afraid the sentries will hear us. We'll have to wait till later and hope they go away.'

After an hour or more one of the doors was opened and four soldiers entered, carrying pots of water and some loaves of bread. They were taking no chances, for other soldiers stood by the door with muskets at the ready.

'Here's your supper, lads,' said the leading soldier. 'Make the most of it, for you won't get more till Sherborne.'

They dumped the things on the earth, went out and barred the door again. We all pushed forward till one of the older men said, 'Steady, steady on. Let's divide it up fairly, so everyone gets his share.'

At that we stood back a bit, and let him divide the bread between us.

'Go easy on the water,' he said. 'Let everyone have a drink, but better keep some for later.'

The bread was rather dry, but it and the water did make us feel better. After eating Matthew and I went to the doors and peeped through cracks, and could see no sign of the sentries on either side. We rattled the doors and roused no shouts, so came to the conclusion that the sentries had gone for their supper, or maybe were going to leave us alone all night while they found somewhere comfortable to sleep. No doubt they thought we were securely imprisoned.

At once we set to work with the iron bar, attacking the wall in a place where the plaster had already fallen off and a crack went quite deeply into the wall. It was hard work and we took turns. We seemed to make a lot of noise, though it probably sounded louder inside the barn than without. We were probably helped by the fact that a cow, doubtless one whose calf had been taken away, kept mooing loudly late into the night. There was a strong wind, too, that made the doors of a nearby stable swing and slam.

We also had some luck in that when the soldiers did come to check on us we happened to have ceased digging for a moment. We were just passing the iron bar to a fresh digger when we heard someone outside trying the doors. We kept quiet, and heard footsteps in the yard, and in a short while the doors on the other side were also rattled. There was then the sound of someone stumbling and swearing—he had evidently tripped over something in the dark. We waited for some time, but heard only the mooing of the cow and the banging of the stable door, and came to the conclusion that a sentry had come to check that we were secure, and then gone away.

We had to risk that he might come back, and commenced digging again. Once we had burrowed some way into the wall it seemed easier. Perhaps the core had not been compacted so hard as the outside. But it was long after midnight when we first thrust the bar through the outer plaster and felt the cold night air blowing in through our hole. It did not take long then to enlarge it enough for a man to squeeze through, and we lost no time in doing that. Man after man wriggled through the hole, those already out helping by pulling the arms of those struggling through. There was a moment of anxiety when a particularly large man seemed to have got stuck, but by vigorous pulling combined with a push from behind we got him through, and presently everyone was out.

There was some moonlight, though behind thin clouds, giving us enough light to pick our way. We had a whispered discussion which way to go. Some wanted to strike out further away from Cerne and over the hill to Sydling to the west, and back to

Dorchester by a round-about route, arguing that the enemy would not expect them to go that way. Others proposed creeping through Cerne itself and up to the ridge beyond, which would lead directly home. Others, including Matthew and me, thought that in the dark it would be best to keep to the road we had come, and go back along the river valley, but be prepared to take to the hills if pursued.

So we split into several parties, and moved off as quietly as we could. The group I was with found our way to the crossroads at the outskirts of Cerne, where we turned right, while the half dozen or so who were going to risk going through the village went straight on. We saw no sign of soldiers, and hoped they were all fast asleep, perhaps having found accommodation in the village.

But we had not gone more than a quarter of a mile before we heard a lot of barking from that direction. The group going through the village had not reckoned on the watch-dogs and had disturbed them, and thus put us all in danger.

I was told afterwards that when the dogs started barking our people ran for all they were worth, no doubt stumbling in the dark and causing more noise. However, they all got through the village safely and climbed the hill above the abbey ruins. They were thus somewhat north-east of the village, away from the direction the Cavaliers would expect them to go, and probably for this reason they were not found, and eventually all returned home safely.

But their folly in taking the route they did had roused the soldiers, some of whom probably went in various directions over the fields in search of them, but others must have run to the barn and found our hole and that we had escaped. It took a little while for them to saddle their horses and set off to find us, but all too soon that is what they did. Fortunately they made so much noise that we had good warning of what they were doing. There were twenty or more in our party, and we hid in a ditch as the horsemen approached. We cowered down and saw them passing as great dark shadows against the sky. Their clatter faded away towards Godmanstone, and we had a whispered conference about what we should do.

'If they don't find us by the time they get to Godmanstone I think they'll come back, or maybe ride up to the hills on either side and search the ridgeways,' I said. 'At anyrate they'll know we can't have gone further than that in the time, and will come back to search more thoroughly.'

'I think we should split up into twos or threes,' said Matthew. 'Then it will be easier to hide, and if any are found they won't catch us all.'

We agreed with that, and crept away in small groups, disappearing into the darkness. Matthew and I went together, and I was pleased at how sensibly he was facing our difficulties and dangers.

'I think we should leave the road,' I said, and we pushed through a hedge and out onto the open downs.

We struck out at an angle to the road, going south-west up the side of the hill. The moon was almost setting, and was often hidden by fast-moving clouds, so it was not easy to see where we were putting our feet, and we made but slow progress. We must have been somewhere above Godmanstone when we heard horses trotting on the road below us, but could not see them. We went on a little further, and soon the light of early dawn was beginning to show.

'Before it gets too light we'd better find somewhere to hide,' I said. 'If they call off the search, well and good—we can go on in daylight. But if they're still hunting for us we'll have to wait till night.'

The open downland did not provide many places for concealment, so when we chanced upon an old haystack left over from last year and partly broken down, we stopped to consider it.

I said it was too obvious a hiding place, but Matthew pointed out that apart from it there were no hiding places at all as far as we could see. So with some misgivings we managed to climb on top of the stack and burrowed into the hay. which was somewhat musty, but warm and restful after our exertions.

We lay and dozed until it was full daylight. Larks were singing and the sun was shining. We peeped out and had a view along the hill the way we had come in the dark. The downland was scattered with sheep, but there were no people to be seen, not even a shepherd-boy. We decided to wait a bit longer in case the Cavaliers came looking for us.

While we lay there we talked about our hopes for the future, supposing we succeeded in getting home safely.

I mentioned that I was thinking of looking for a helper in my shop.

'Do you think I could do it?' Matthew asked eagerly. 'I would do my best to learn.'

'If you really want to be an apothecary you ought to be properly apprenticed,' I said, 'and I'm not sure that I'm wanting an apprentice or am willing to take on that extra responsibility as yet, though in time that may come. But if you were willing to come as an assistant, and see how you—or rather we—get along, I would teach you as much as would be necessary, and you could find out if that is really what you want to do in life. But what would your father say?'

'I would have to talk to him, of course, but I don't think he would object to my trying the work. He thinks highly of you, Mr Judd, I believe.'

'What makes you think that?' I asked.

'I mentioned to him that I had been talking to you, and he said, "Mr Judd is a man worth knowing", so he must think well of you.'

'Ah, that is because I support Parliament, not because of my merits,' I said with a laugh.

'So what do you say, Mr Judd? May I come and work for you?'

'Supposing we get home again safely, which is still somewhat doubtful, yes, we will try the arrangement. If it works, well and good, and if not there will be no hard feelings I trust.'

'Look out, sir!' Matthew grasped my arm. 'Look there, someone's coming!'

I turned to where he was pointing and saw that some sheep were running in panic, and a moment later two horsemen came into view galloping over the downs. Soon we could make out that they were soldiers, and we shrank back into the hay.

They rode up to our stack and stopped so close that we could hear them talking.

'This is the sort of place they might hide,' said one.

'Nah,' said the other, 'they didn't come up this far, or at anyrate we haven't seen a trace of 'em. They're more likely heading for Dorchester.'

'That'll be up the hill on the other side,' agreed his mate. 'But let's pull the hay down a bit to make sure.'

'No, come on,' said the other. 'I want me breakfast,' and we heard him trotting away. His companion got off his horse and was quiet, and I wondered whether he was listening for us or contemplating where to pull at the hay. But then he mounted his horse again and rode off after the other, so we decided that he must have simply been relieving himself against the stack.

After that we stayed in the hay for some time longer, in case other soldiers might be searching. By about mid morning we had seen no more of them, and thought it would be safe to go on. So we slid down the stack and set off south along the ridge. We were both feeling hungry and thirsty, but up here on the downs there were no cottages or brooks, so we had to bear our wants as patiently as we could.

We plodded across Charminster Down, and descended gradually towards the valley. At last we neared a farmhouse and paused to examine it carefully before we approached, to make sure that no soldiers were there. The dogs barked as we went into the yard, and the farmer's wife looked out.

'You poor things,' she said, 'you look as if you've fallen in a ditch.'

We asked her if she had seen any soldiers.

'Early this morning,' she told us, 'two of those devils came riding up and said they were looking for deserters. I told 'em to search the barns if they wished, but we had none such here. But they didn't bother, for I think they were tired, and had decided to give up the search, for I heard one say they had better be on their way or they would miss their companions going to Sherborne.'

She gave us a drink and some bread and cheese to eat, and after a little rest we thanked her heartily and continued on our way. As we approached the village of Charminster we went warily, but saw no sign of soldiers, so walked on through the village and joined the upper Sherborne road. There we met two more of our party who had spent the night hiding in a thicket, so went on together and came down to Dorchester. We entered the town safely, and were welcomed by no less a person than the Mayor.

'Were you among those taken by Lord Hopton?' he asked. 'It was a disgrace, a gross violation of our hospitality. I shall send a protest to the King in the strongest terms.'

'Have any of the others got back safely?' I asked.

'Yes, thank God. About forty were taken, I believe, and more than half have already reached home safely. They have told us how you escaped from the barn. An excellent thing, excellent!'

I went on down to Durn Lane and my home, where Agnes greeted me with a mixture of joy at my safe return and blame for the anxiety she had suffered.

'You told me you weren't going to run into danger again,' she said. 'What would I do if you were taken away or killed? What would happen to little Mark or the new babe? How can you say you love me when you do this to me?'

'But dearest,' I said, 'this time it wasn't my fault for putting myself in danger. I was seized while walking peacefully along the highway. One is not safe anywhere now, it seems. But at least I have come back safe and sound.'

'Look at your clothes! That's another doublet and breeches ruined! Oh, Micah, why can't you keep out of danger? I hate you, I do, I hate you!'

Then she flung her arms round me and kissed me. Really, I don't understand women. But she was right, my clothes were in a state, and I needed to look sober and reliable when I visited Mr Barton, which I must shortly do.

Chapter 9 Contrasting conspirators

AFTER A WASH and change of clothes and a meal I felt better. But with all these absences I felt that my business would suffer, and I was glad I had agreed with Matthew that he would come as my assistant. However, that would have to wait, because I had messages to pass on that had already been too long delayed. So after eating and hearing from Agnes of several people who needed visits, and looking at things in the shop, I went to see Mr Barton.

He welcomed me much more warmly than before, and I knew why when he said how his son had told him about our adventures, and had evidently painted in glowing colours my part in the escape.

'Thank God, if he had to be conscripted in that barbarous fashion, that Matthew was with you,' he said. 'It would have broken my heart if he had been forced to fight for the King and that damnable Lord Hopton. And my wife was nearly beside herself with worry when he didn't come home. We heard how men had been taken off the streets, and feared the worst. But of course we knew nothing for certain.'

'I'm glad it ended well,' I said. 'Has Matthew said anything else to you about me?'

'No, what should he have said?'

'He will speak to you soon, I expect,' I said. 'But have you heard whether the rest of our people who were conscripted got home safely?'

'Praise the Lord, many of them have,' he said. 'But I believe some are still unaccounted for. However, it is nonethe less a singular mercy to us all, and a shame upon the enemy.'

'Thank God indeed,' I said. 'But all this affair has seriously delayed important news. Indeed, yesterday I was on my way back here to tell you the tidings, when I was so outrageously seized by

Lord Hopton's men.'

'The plague! What news? My worries about Matthew had quite put other matters out of my mind.'

'Lord Essex is coming. The messenger arrived yesterday, and the news is that his lordship has made up his mind to leave his position watching the king, and come as we hoped to take Weymouth. He will move as fast as he can, I expect, and could be here in Dorchester in a day or two.'

'Oh Lord,' he said, 'what is to be done? This is so very sudden.'

'I know, and I am sorry the intelligence did not reach you yesterday. But it's not too late to act upon it, and now will be your chance if you are thinking of taking over the town.'

'This hardly gives us time. Really we are not ready. Heaven help me, I must think what to do.'

'But I thought you had everything in hand,' I said, 'or was it all words and imaginings?'

'No, no,' he protested, 'we do have it all in hand. But we are not ready to strike "in a day or two". We need longer to prepare. However, I will see what can be done. Let me think—I will go at once and confer with the others. Perhaps we will at least be able to arrange for our people to be in charge of the gates and to be patrolling the walls when Lord Essex comes, so that he is not prevented from entering.'

'Well, I have given you the news, and must leave you to make of it what you can,' I said. 'But I must go now, for I must pass on the news to the others.'

Clearly the conspirators in Melcombe and Weymouth must be told as soon as possible, and I felt I must go there myself, for it was too important to trust to anyone else, although I did not relish the prospect of seeing Mr Webb and his two 'mastiffs' again. But I felt disappointed in Mr Barton. Of what use was courage and of all the efforts I and others had made, and of Lady Alicia's bravery, if his inefficiency and lethargy allowed opportunities like this to pass unseized? I just hoped Mr Webb would be better prepared.

Back home I saddled my horse and, after a brief word with Agnes to explain where I was going, rode out on the Weymouth road. I felt I was beginning to know every bush and pothole on that way, with the gradual slope down until near the Monkton turning, then the longer slope up towards the Ridgeway. Then came the wide view from the top, with the sea stretching right and left and Portland grey and solid in the distance. Soon I was plunging down the steep hill, and thought of Malachy as I passed the turning to Upwey, and wondered again how Sir James might be brought to justice.

At least my capture by Lord Hopton's men, and my talk with the soldier, had enabled me to find out definite news of Sir James's part in telling the Cavaliers about Roundhead plots. But I was still just as far from knowing whether he or Webb, or maybe some unknown person, had killed Godwin. Perhaps when Lord Essex arrived it might be possible to make further inquiries and even persuade Essex to have Sir James brought in for questioning. As for Mr Webb, if his scheme for handing over Weymouth to the Roundheads succeeded I supposed he would be too much in favour for me to get Lord Essex to take any action against him. Not that I wanted anyone to be punished for Godwin's death: I simply hoped I might learn enough to save Malachy from execution.

I passed the sentry post, and was relieved to find that there were still no soldiers there. Evidently news of Essex's move had not yet reached the garrison. Finally I found my way to the back street and Mr Webb's yard. I left my horse there, climbed the steps and knocked on the door.

There could not have been a greater contrast than that between the plotters of Dorchester and Weymouth. One of the big bodyguards opened the door, and ushered me into Mr Webb's presence.

'Good day to you, Mr Judd,' he said briskly. 'I got your message with the pills and understood that Lord Essex was going to confer with another general—Waller, I guessed. But what was this about an infection and Mr Sutler?'

'Our messenger to Lord Essex came upon this Mr Sutler, (a

most dangerous and dishonest fellow, it seems), and discovered that he was carrying a letter from Sir James Freke and a list of names, apparently of your Weymouth band here. At all events, your name and Mr Horner's were on it, as was Mr Godwin's. So I fear you have been betrayed, though whether Sir James has been shown the list I do not know.'

'I have met that Sutler,' said Webb, 'and did not trust him. How he came by the list of our names I don't know, but I fear there may be traitors in our midst—or maybe the one traitor, as I told you before. What became of this list?'

'I have it at home. Our messenger took from Mr Sutler's pocket.'

'A resourceful fellow, that messenger!' Mr Webb exclaimed.

'Indeed, sir, most resourceful,' I agreed, and did not tell him the messenger's sex.

'However,' he continued, 'I don't think Sir James can have seen it, otherwise the Cavaliers would have taken measures against us. But in any case if we can act quickly all will be well. Has Lord Essex made a decision to come to our aid?'

'He has—he's on his way, and may be in Dorset already.' I explained to him how I had been delayed in passing on the news.

'No matter,' he said, 'we are ready. Our plans to take Weymouth and the Chapel Fort are all in hand, and just await the moment and the word. Sandsfoot Castle will have to be left for Lord Essex's army. He will come with some heavy guns I hope, so that he can subdue it. Let's think—if Lord Essex enters Dorset today or tomorrow, he could be here in four days if he bestirs himself. I would like the attack to take place next Lord's Day, if he can get here by then, for on that day the soldiers will mostly be off duty, and not expecting us to strike.'

'He will have to come through Dorchester,' I said, 'and will take another day to get to you. You could confer with him when he gets to us, and make final arrangements for him to join his attack with yours.'

'Yes,' he agreed, 'we must certainly confer with him about the timing, for if he comes too early the garrison will be alerted and bar his approach, and also prevent our rising. In such a case Lord Essex would have to fight his way in, and might not succeed.'

'He will not be willing to settle here for a long siege,' I said. 'As it is, he is defying Parliament by coming here, and only the prospect of a quick victory has persuaded him to do so. If he can present them with a triumph and the twin towns here are seized from the Cavaliers, all will be well; but he is taking a gamble none the less.'

'All the more reason for making sure his approach will tie in with our rising,' said Webb. 'But as soon as the garrison get wind of his coming into Dorset they will no doubt guard the ways in and out of town, which will make it difficult for us to come and see the Earl.'

'If they know of his approach surely they will also prevent your rising?'

'On the contrary, they will be arranging all their forces to resist an attack from outside. They believe they have foiled our plans and that our people are in disarray, so I trust we will take them entirely by surprise.'

'What has persuaded them that you are no longer a danger?' I asked.

'The death of George Godwin. It turned out fortunate for us, though not of course for him. But they thought that he was the prime mover of our plans, as he was the nominal head of our band, though I (you understand, I am sure) have always been the actual leader. But Godwin's death, they suppose, has thrown us into utter confusion.'

'They will still be extra alert, I should have thought, when Essex comes near.'

'I think not,' he said. 'They will not know where he is heading. They will hear that he has entered the county, but will be quite uncertain where he intends to proceed. Even when he gets to

Dorchester it will still be doubtful that he will attack Weymouth, and we will put about that he is to take the Bridport road with the aim of relieving the siege of Lyme, which is what the Cavaliers will anyway expect him to do. If he then sends a troop of horse here ahead of his main body they should still achieve surprise and catch the enemy before they are aware, though I hope by that time we shall have secured the main strong-points.'

'Then what you will need to arrange with Essex is exactly when you want him to dispatch his cavalry. He will need to know your plans and and how much backing you will want and at what time.'

'Absolutely,' he said, 'that is well and truly put. You see the situation clearly. Who could better explain the plan to him than yourself? Would you do that?'

'What would you want me to say?'

'Tell him we plan to seize the strong-points in both Melcombe and Weymouth at the same moment on the morning of the day. We must of course agree on a particular day and keep to it. If all goes well, we shall disarm some of the enemy and drive the rest back up to Sandsfoot Castle. If things go badly in Weymouth we will pull up the drawbridge and wait in Melcombe for help, but I hope we shall be able to hand over both towns to Lord Essex when he arrives. His troops will be needed to repel any counter-attack, and to bottle up the enemy in the Castle until it can be taken.'

'I understand,' I said, 'so tell me, when exactly will you want the horsemen to arrive? What do you want me to propose to Lord Essex?'

'Ask him to send his troops to arrive by, say, mid-morning on the day. I should think by half past nine or ten o'clock we should have secured the the towns if we are going to. Put to him that the Lord's Day, Sunday, would be the best, supposing he arrives in time for that. In any case can you let us know in some way which day he will be coming?'

'Yes, I think I can,' I said. 'I have an idea. Look, you can see the ridge on the way to Dorchester from here, and even the notch in the summit where the road comes over it. As soon as Lord Essex arrives I will go to him and explain your plan. Then I will ride out to the ridge and light a fire or fires. One column of smoke will mean he is coming one day after the signal, two columns two days, and so on.'

'Let us be clear about it,' said Mr Webb, 'if, say, on Saturday we see one column of smoke it will mean that his troops will be here on Sunday morning, whereas two would mean Monday morning.'

'Agreed,' I said, 'whichever day you see the smoke, count the number of fires to see how many days after that Lord Essex's troops will come. And for his encouragement, can I assure him that when his horsemen approach Melcombe they will meet no opposition?'

'I cannot absolutely guarantee that, for there are always chances in war. But if it is humanly possible, and with the help of the Lord, I will see to it.'

He nodded, shook my hand, then signed to the guard to show me out.

As I rode back up the Dorchester road I thought, Mr Webb is not a likeable man. He is harsh and cold. But if I were in a fight I would rather have him in charge than many more amiable characters.

As I had seen no soldiers and had no trouble on my way to Weymouth I did not anticipate any on my way home. So I was given an unpleasant shock when, as I approached the guard-post which had earlier been deserted, two soldiers leapt out in front of me. One of them was waving a pistol and shouted 'Hold!'.

I suppose I might have spurred my horse and galloped past and hoped that he would miss, but as I had nothing to hide it seemed safer to obey him and stop.

'Who are you, and where are you going?' demanded the man with the pistol. He was, I guess, a corporal.

'Micah Judd, apothecary of Dorchester, on my way home.'

'And what is your business in Weymouth?'

'Seeing one of my people in this town. An apothecary, as I

hope you realise, has to travel far to see sick folk.'

'Not as far as this, surely! Let me see your pass.'

''Fore God!' I said, 'I am a free-born Englishman going about my lawful business. I do not need a pass.'

'No pass, no passage,' he said.

I was wondering what to do when the other man spoke.

'That's a fine horse you've got, far too fine a mount for an apothecary.'

'Yea,' said the corporal, 'too fine by half. I think we'll have him. Get down, apothecary.'

'Oh sir,' I said, 'I need a horse for my work. How could I get around to the many sick folk who rely upon me if I did not have a horse. How could I go as far as I need to gather herbs? A horse is absolutely necessary to me.'

'Pah! Our need is greater than yours,' he said, 'and I know of apothecaries who manage on foot. We'll have no more argument—get down.'

'Well, sir, if I must, please help me. For I shall be in great trouble if I give up my horse without seeming to have had a struggle. All my friends will mock me. Could you make it appear as if I put up a fight? Could you please send a bullet through my hat.'

I held out my hat at arm's length, and he obliged by discharging his pistol at it. I kicked my horse's sides and galloped away with their curses ringing in my ears, and was well out of range before he could reload.

I smiled as I waved my hat at them from a safe distance, but resolved to take more care in future, for the loss of my horse would have been a disaster for me. However, I reached home without further adventures.

Next morning I called on Tom Hartley, to ask him to make me a new doublet and breeches, for those I had been wearing when I escaped from Cerne were too badly torn to mend.

'What, Micah,' he exclaimed, another suit of clothes! You keep me in business, I think.'

I told him about my being taken by the Cavaliers, and impressed as a soldier.

'I have heard about that,' he said, 'but didn't know you were involved. All I heard was that every single man that was taken reached home safely.'

'I'm glad to hear that, for I was afraid some of us might have been recaptured.'

'Tell me exactly what happened. Please, I want to know all about it.'

So I told him all the details of our adventures from the moment I was caught on the way back from Wolfeton, our breaking out of the barn, and our narrow escape on the downs. He was very impressed, and I could see he was eager to tell all his other friends what had happened.

'And what news have you, Tom?' I asked him.

'Well now, they say that Lyme is still holding out, though 'tis feared they have had many killed.'

'And what news in the town here?'

'Most of the talk is still about that he-witch. And I must warn you, Micah, I have heard your name mentioned by several of our fellow-citizens as someone associated with him. You had better keep well away from that man. 'Tis dangerous to go near him.'

I certainly did not like what I heard, and went back to my shop wondering how I could help Malachy without damaging my own reputation, or indeed putting my own life in danger.

Later that morning Matthew Barton came to see me, and said that he had spoken to his father, and (after what I understood had been a rather difficult interview) had his permission to work for me for a trial period. So at once I set him to work, washing bottles and pounding herbs in the mortar. I was pleased to see that he set about the chores without grumbling, and in turn over a number of days I gradually explained to him something of an apothecary's work, and why the various operations had to be done.

'Some herbs will keep,' I explained, 'especially if they have been carefully prepared. But these roots you are bruising are for a decoction and are for immediate use.'

One day I showed him how I boiled the bruised roots over my charcoal brazier until the water was reduced, allowed it to cool, then strained it through a cloth, added some sugar, bottled and labelled it, and put it ready to take to a patient. Another time I showed him how to make pills, and which were the medicines I found of most use for the commonest ailments. It would not be long, I felt, before I could at least leave Matthew in charge of the shop when I had to be away.

In fact he wanted to learn faster than would have been good for him. He asked about the gathering of herbs, and whether it was important to seek them at particular times.

'That will come later,' I said. 'When you have learnt what to do with a few simple remedies will be time enough to think about gathering. You really need to know a lot about the stars, and which (when they are in the ascendant) are fortunate or unfortunate; and which will strengthen and which weaken the powers of the herbs. Also,' I went on, 'each part of the body has its particular governor, whether planet or star, and one needs to match the medicine not only to the disease but also to the bodily part by the laws of astrology.'

'Oh, Mr Judd,' he said, 'you make my head whirl. I hope to learn all these things eventually, but I can see that it will take time.'

'Don't worry,' I said, 'you can sell most of the common remedies to people, and they will do some good and no harm, without having to know all about their horoscopes.'

In these sorts of ways I taught him bit by bit, and he made good progress.

A day or two after he began to work for me he was minding the shop while I was fetching a bag of herbs I had left in the stable. I was just coming back through the door when I heard someone enter from the lane and give a sharp exclamation, even perhaps an oath.

'What the devil are you doing here?' said a harsh voice, and I saw a big well-dressed man had paused half inside the street door. It was Rachel's father, Mr Haggard.

When he saw me he came right into the shop.

'Ah, are you Mr Judd?' he said in a more friendly tone. 'I nearly didn't come in when I saw who you have assisting you.'

'Mr Haggard,' I said, my colour rising, for I thought his rudeness intolerable, 'if you have come to buy something it should not matter who is serving you, provided my ointment or whatever it is is of good quality, which it will be. But if you have come to see me, I can take you inside for a private conversation, if you wish.'

'I am sorry,' he said. 'I should not have spoken as I did. But this young man's father has insulted me in the public street, and I loathe his politics and his religion.'

'Come now, Mr Haggard,' I said, not wanting to excite him further, though I could have pointed out that he had been just as insulting to Mr Barton, 'whatever your quarrel with the father, you should have no quarrel with his son. Matthew is a good worker and a staunch fellow, so please may we leave it at that.'

'That may be so, but I have a further quarrel with this young man,' he replied. 'I have forbidden my daughter and him to have any meeting or communication, and I strongly suspect that they are disobeying me.'

Matthew, who had been standing looking from one to the other as we talked, was about to protest then, but I forestalled him, for I could see the dispute would become more heated if he did.

'Mr Haggard, come through to my parlour and have a glass of wine with me, if you will, for I have something to tell you in private. If you would mind the shop for me, Matthew.'

Mr Haggard hesitated, and I thought he was going to refuse, but as Matthew restrained himself and drew back into a corner, and I held the inner door open, he gave a kind of shrug and accepted my invitation. Agnes was in the parlour with little Mark, and meeting her in her neat house-dress and with her pleasant smile further mollified him.

Having greeted him she took Mark into the kitchen to Hester. I invited Mr Haggard to sit down and poured us each a glass of my mother-in-law's cowslip wine.

'Now sir,' I said, sitting down opposite him, 'you came to my shop not (I am sure) to annoy yourself with the sight of my young helper. Did you want some medicine, or to see me?'

'Mr Judd, sir, I thank you for this excellent wine, and I apologise again for my outburst. But I had no idea that I should find that young fellow working for you, and the sight of him was too much. You see, sir, I need some cordial for my wife, and I came to your shop rather than to old Wellworthy's because my daughter recommended you. I gather that she had been to shop here, and I fear that I now understand why. If indeed I find that she has been coming to see this fellow, I shall have to take severe measures, for I strictly forbade her to have any dealings with him.'

'No no, Mr Haggard,' I raised a hand in protest, 'she came quite innocently some while ago, and has not been here since Matthew started to work for me. He's only been here for a day or two. And truly, sir, you must not visit the sins of the father upon the son. I do beg you to judge Matthew for himself. He's a brave and capable young man.'

'That may be,' he said, finishing his wine and putting the glass on the table, 'but I do not wish my family to be associated with his. His father is a leader amongst those who have rebelled against our lawful church and king. I cannot stand the man!'

'Sir, sir!' I said, fearing he was working himself into a passion again, 'will you have some more wine?'

'No no, thank you, I must be going.'

'Wait one moment, sir, and let me tell you a true story. It will explain how Matthew comes to be working for me. It was when we were hiding in a haystack in fear for our lives.'

I told him how we had been taken away by Lord Hopton's men. He had heard of that, of course, but did not know the particulars. I emphasised Matthew's part in our escape, and how brave and level-headed he had shown himself. I described our hiding in the haystack, and how Matthew had asked to come and work for me, and how well he was doing.

I was a little afraid that Mr Haggard, as a Royalist, might feel that we ought to have gone on to fight in the king's army, but I hoped that as a Dorchester man he would be outraged by what had been done to us.

And so he was.

'It was disgraceful taking you like that,' he said, 'and your escape was most creditable. Yes, I will grant you that Matthew sounds a staunch fellow, and I could wish he was on the right side in our sad divisions. But I still cannot contemplate a union between my family and his. If his father were less of a bigot I might consider it, but as things are...' He left the rest unsaid, and rose to his feet.

'At least, sir,' I said as I went to open the door to the shop, 'let Matthew serve you this morning. I have an excellent cordial, which I think your wife will like.'

'Oh, very well,' he said, and I was pleased to see him ask Matthew for the cordial quite politely and pleasantly. Fearing that Matthew might think of saying more on the subject of Rachel, and thereby stirring Mr Haggard's wrath again, I shook my head at him and he kept silent. I believe Mr Haggard had also expected Matthew to plead with him, and was pleasantly surprised when he didn't.

'There! You see how set he is against me,' Matthew exclaimed, as the street door closed behind him. 'Why is he so—' He paused.

'Bigoted?' I suggested. 'That is what he thinks your father is. But I've put in a good word for you, so don't despair. Little by little you may win him over.'

Certainly I felt some progress had been made in that direction. What advance the plot was making was another matter. I could not hurry it, and could only hope that Lord Essex would soon appear—or at least send word.

Chapter 10 Lord Essex

FRIDAY CAME, just over a week after Lord Essex had met Waller at Stow-on-the-Wold, and four days since Lady Alicia's man had arrived back with the news, and we still had no knowledge of whether the Roundhead army had entered Dorset. Indeed it seemed to me that Parliament might have been so insistent that Essex must stay to watch the King that he could have changed his mind again, in which case all our plans in Dorchester and Weymouth would come to nothing.

Nevertheless Mr Barton did cultivate friendship with the Captain of Militia in Dorchester, and managed to arrange that mainly Parliamentary supporters, or at least those who were sympathetic to the Cause, were on duty at the gates for the next few days. Others, more Royalist-inclined, were put to patrolling the walls if they weren't off duty.

Especially staunch men were put in charge of East Gate on this Friday, which turned out to be a very fortunate thing. They were commanded by none other than my friend Joel Andrews the tanner, who had always been inclined to support Parliament. Our experiences of late, while the Cavaliers had control of Dorchester, had made him more forthright against them.

Early in the afternoon a group of horsemen were seen galloping down the hill towards the water-meadows. The look-out at the Gate was alert, and saw the sunlight glinting on their helmets and breastplates and called to Joel:

'There's so'jers in armour gallopin' this way!'

'Shut an' bar the gates,' shouted Joel.

The men jumped to it, the gates thudded shut, the great wooden beams were slid into place behind them, and one of the watch was dispatched up East Street into town to warn the Mayor.

A little while later the leaders of the troop, which seemed to fill the road as far as one could see—there must have been over a thousand of them—arrived before the Gate.

'Open up in the King's name!' shouted the Captain.

'Who are you?' asked Joel.

'Soldiers of the King,' came the reply. 'We're being pursued—we've been chased all the way from Blandford by the Roundheads, curse 'em! Lord Essex's men very devils they are!—so let us in.'

'No sir,' said Joel, 'you'll have to go elsewhere.'

'God damme!' swore the Captain, 'isn't Dorchester now a loyal town? Haven't you submitted to His Majesty?'

'You're not comin' in here,' said Joel.

'But God in heaven, don't you realise that Lord Essex is in Blandford, only twenty miles away? You'll need us to help in your defence.'

'You're not comin' in,' repeated Joel.

'Oh for heaven's sake!' said the Captain, 'blast and damn you to hell! You'll suffer for this! But come on, men, we can't loiter here. On, then, to Sherborne.'

And they turned their horses and cut across the north of the water-meadows to join the Sherborne road. We heard afterwards that there had been over fifteen hundred of them, including some French mercenaries, who had been surprised near Blandford by four hundred of Essex's cavalry. They had been seized with panic and hadn't been able to stop until they reached Dorchester, although Essex's men had long since given up the chase.

At all events, Joel was praised by all except rabid Cavaliers for his firmness, for even most of the Royalists in the town wouldn't have wanted to accommodate all those horsemen. Also, when they thought over the matter, the more knowledgeable among them realised that cavalry would have been of little use in defending the walls, especially men who were so easily put to flight.

But the incident was particularly encouraging for us who knew what had been planned, in that it assured us that Essex was on his way, and could be in Dorchester on the morrow. The prospect put Mr Barton into a flutter.

'Whatever are we to do now?' he asked, when I went to ask him what he was arranging for Essex's arrival.

'What about the Royalists here, men like William Churchill?' I said. 'I'm not suggesting that you arrest them, but we ought to make sure they don't hinder Lord Essex's entry.'

'Oh yes, yes indeed. We'll make certain we have true men in charge of the gates. But what to do with the Royalists—I think we'll leave the Earl to deal with them.'

Really Mr Barton was not much good as a conspirator, but when I considered how feebly all the rest of the townspeople of Dorchester had managed when the Cavaliers came last year I doubted whether any others of us would have done better. And maybe Mr Barton's lack of ruthlessness in taking action against his opponents (in striking contrast to his words) was typical of what made Dorchester a good and mostly peaceful place to live.

So it came about that next day, although everyone in town knew that the Roundheads were approaching, and some were glad and some fearful, there was no violence, and people of opposing opinions tended to avoid one another rather than having arguments or blows. But remembering what we had suffered at the hands of Prince Maurice's troops a few months before made people anxious, and many of us again hid our money and treasures. I had made a hiding place with a stout box under a stone in my yard, and now put in it all my spare cash and my few bits of silver and Agnes's jewels.

It was just after midday that a troop of horse was seen coming down the Blandford road towards the River Frome. The watchers at the East Gate raised the alarm and shut the gate, but when it was certain that these were Lord Essex's advance guard the gates were opened, and Lord Essex himself was seen riding along just behind them. The leading horsemen rode in and lined the street while Essex and his staff officers entered the town. He was met by the Mayor, and I noticed that our Royalist Deputy Governor, William Churchill, and his Lieutenant, Joseph Paty, were both absent, probably wisely, although Lord Essex was a more tolerant man than many on either side.

I watched as the Earl rode up East Street. He had long rather untidy bushy hair, a short pointed beard and a big moustache with ends that curled up very fashionably over his cheeks. He was in armour, with a fine lace collar falling over his shoulders, and had a long straight sword in the scabbard at his side. He was riding a handsome grey horse. He looked tired and dusty after his ride, and went straight to his lodgings at the Earl of Bedford's house in the High Street, which is where visiting dignitaries usually seem to stay. To our great relief most of his men bivouacked in fields outside the town, and were generally well-behaved, though some of our people complained afterwards that they had been robbed.

As soon as the Earl was settled and had had time to eat and rest a little, I went to his lodging to see him. But this proved harder than I expected. The sentry at the door would neither let me in nor take a message for me. His lordship was tired and not to be disturbed, he said.

This was very frustrating, because it was essential for the success of the plot to capture Weymouth that the Earl should agree to send his forces at the right moment, and I needed to have time to ride to the ridge to signal to the plotters. But how was I to get to talk with the Earl and arrange matters?

Then I had an idea. Perhaps if Lady Alicia came and demanded access she would be allowed to go in and see him, and then she could ask him to send for me. As every minute could be vital I decided to go to her with all speed, and hurried home to saddle my horse. I rode swiftly to Wolfeton, and fortunately found the Lady at home. Soon I was explaining my difficulty to her.

'The silly man,' she said. 'He is like to endanger his whole reason for defying Parliament and coming to Dorset if he won't see you. Of course I'll come at once.'

She started calling servants, and within a quarter of an hour was on her horse accompanying me back to Dorchester.

'I shall go in, for I am sure they won't be able to keep me out, and explain to Uncle Robert—Lord Essex—just how important it is that he should see you at once,' she said. 'You wait outside, Mr Judd, and I warrant you in five minutes I'll have you in!' Her eyes lit up at the thought, and in her confidence I found my worries disappearing.

We rode down the street and dismounted outside the Earl of Bedford's house. A couple of boys came forward eager to earn a tip by holding our horses.

Lady Alicia went up to the sentry and gave him a dazzling smile.

'Good afternoon, my man,' she said, 'would you kindly tell Lord Essex that Lady Alicia has come to pay her respects.'

'He's seeing no one, ma'am,' he said.

'Nonsense, man, Uncle Robert will see me. Go and tell him I am here.'

'I can't leave my post, ma'am.'

'Then have the goodness to call an attendant,' she said imperiously, though with another winning smile.

'Right, m'lady,' he said, and called in through the door.

A corporal appeared.

'No visitors,' he said, 'his lordship is not to be disturbed.'

'Oh, but he will see me. I am Lady Alicia and he is my uncle,' she said, and swept past him into the hall. He shrugged his shoulders, pulled a face at the sentry, and followed her, and I heard her in ringing tones telling him to look sharp and tell the Earl she was waiting.

After about ten minutes during which I tried to engage the sentry in conversation without success, the corporal reappeared looking rather sulky and beckoned me to enter. He led me up the stairs, and at the top I found Lady Alicia about to come down.

'He will see you, Mr Judd,' she said. 'I have told him the whole success of his expedition depends upon you!'

I thanked her for her help, and as I followed the corporal into a room across the landing she went down the stairs.

Lord Essex was half lying on a bed, with his boots off. One foot was stretched out on the bed, the other on the floor. He was now in his mid fifties, I believe, and had been campaigning since the beginning of the war. Indeed he had been a soldier for much longer and, as Lady Alicia had mentioned, had fought on the continent and learnt his soldiering there. Close to I could see that his face was looking old and lined. No doubt he was tired, but he greeted me civilly enough.

'Come in, Mr Judd. Young Alicia speaks highly of you and tells me that it was you who sent that letter from the people of Weymouth.'

'It was not from me, but was entrusted to me to send on to you, sir.'

'She also says you have something of vital importance to tell me.'

'That is true, my lord,' I replied. 'I have information from our people in Melcombe and Weymouth, and if you agree with their plans, and are willing to send troops when they are needed, I have arranged to signal to them, and they will rise against the garrison as they promised.'

'I have risked my reputation to come at their request,' he said. 'It was but yesterday I received yet another letter from Parliament demanding that I hand over the west country campaign to Sir William Waller and go chasing heaven knows where after the King. But I've told them they must allow me to judge what is needed, or else they can dismiss me from being general. I'm determined to wrest Weymouth from the Cavaliers, even if it's the last thing I do.'

'We are most grateful to you for answering our pleas for help,' I said. 'And now, my lord, with your permission I'll explain what our friends in Melcombe and Weymouth propose to do, and what help they need from you.'

I then outlined the plan, and how they hoped to overpower the garrison, but would leave Sandsfoot Castle for him to conquer.

'They are hoping that their rising will take place on Sunday,' I said, 'for that would catch the garrison unawares, they believe. But they would need your troopers to arrive at the outskirts of Melcombe by about mid-morning, to take over the town and to guard against any counter-attack.'

'But that is tomorrow. I was hoping to give my men time to rest and prepare for battle.'

'I fear, sir, that if there is delay the garrison may take measures which will foil the plot. Could you not at the very least send your cavalry there tomorrow? The greatest hope of success comes from taking the Cavaliers by surprise.'

'True, true,' he said, 'we must strike while the iron is hot, what! But do you think they will really be able to overcome the garrison?'

'If they do achieve surprise I think they will,' I assured him. 'But they will need the backing of your men immediately afterwards to hold the two towns and to confine the surviving enemy in the Castle. But if you can send the troops tomorrow morning, I will let them know at once.'

'How will you communicate with them?'

I told him about the agreed signal.

'Right,' he said. 'Go and light your fire. I think we can manage to gallop up at the time they ask. And you had better come with us, Mr Judd, as we don't want anything to go wrong, or to fall into a trap, or anything like that. Have you got a horse?'

I assured him that I had, and that I would be glad to come, and he told me to report to him in the morning. Finally I asked him to sign a pass for me so that his soldiers would let me go out on the Weymouth road, which he did, and then dismissed me.

I suspected that he did not entirely trust me or the Weymouth conspirators, and that he was going to take me along partly as a hostage. There had been several instances of men offering to betray a garrison and when a force came to take it, betraying the attackers instead. I had heard of at least two incidents like that, where the garrison had been secretly alerted and the attacking forces led into an ambush. It struck me that I knew very little about Mr Webb and his friends, and I could only hope that they were not playing that sort of double game. Certainly if they were, or even if they were sincere but inefficient, and failed to overcome the garrison, my life would not be worth much.

However, I was as sure as I could be that the conspirators were true men and would do their best, and all I could do was to play my part as arranged. So I gathered some kindling, old papers, and small sticks and twigs, and put them in a sack, and took a chopper and a lighted lantern (though I also took tinder, flint and steel, in case of need), and rode out of South Gate. It was a good thing I had got a pass from the Earl, for otherwise the soldiers would not have allowed me through. They were not letting anyone travel that way without a pass, in order, I suppose, to try to prevent news of their presence reaching Weymouth.

I rode up the familiar way, and reached the Ridgeway. Nearby were some thickets of thorn bushes and some wind-stunted trees, and I dismounted beside one and tethered my horse. It was a place of ill-omen for me, for it was there that I had been attacked and robbed just after I met Malachy the first time. I looked around anxiously in case robbers might be lurking behind the bushes; but all was well, I was alone.

I collected sticks and dead branches, and soon had enough, with what I had brought, for a suitable fire. I took an armful of sticks and walked just over the summit, dumped them, then came back for my sack of kindling. Beside the road I set about building a fire with the kindling in the middle and the larger sticks stacked all round. Then from my lantern I lit a strip of paper, and soon had the pile burning. I went back to the thicket and filled the sack with damp dead leaves, and used them to make a good column of smoke which I was sure that the conspirators could not fail to see.

I was glad that there were no other people about, for they might have wanted to know what I was doing. But I did wonder if the fact that no one seemed to be travelling from Weymouth indicated that Essex's arrival in Dorchester was already known there, and that the garrison had been alerted and were perhaps barring the road.

I remounted my horse and rode back home, glancing back from time to time to see the smoke drifting away eastwards. By the time I reached the town it had died away, so I could only hope that its message had been received and would be acted upon. But I could not help fearing that our plans would go wrong. Supposing Lord Essex was about to lead his troops to disaster?

Chapter 11 Rising!

NEXT MORNING, June 16th, Lord's Day, dawned warm and bright, and the church bells were calling people to worship. But we had work to do which the more militant Puritans would no doubt have considered as much the Lord's work as going to pray. The army was astir early, and after a quick breakfast with Agnes I saddled my horse and presented myself at the Earl's lodgings. I was glad to be going with him partly because I always like to see what is going on, and wanted to see how the capture of Melcombe and Weymouth would be managed, but also I thought it might give me the opportunity to ask the Earl to arrest Sir James Freke on suspicion of murder.

As I rode up to the Earl of Bedford's house I saw Lord Essex outside talking to one of his officers whom I did not know, but who (I was later told) was Sir William Balfour, the man appointed to command the horsemen for the initial assault. No doubt Essex was giving him last minute instructions, and I only hoped he would time the attack to fit in effectively with the planned rising.

Lord Essex himself was intending to accompany us, while the main body of troops were to follow as soon as they could. He was already partly armed, and as Sir William trotted off the Earl turned and beckoned me over.

'Did you send the signal as arranged?' he asked.

'Indeed I did, my lord.'

'Good. Now you had better keep to the rear of our party. There you will come to no harm, but be available if I should send for you.'

He gave an order to a sergeant, who told two troopers to accompany me, and they led me to a position near the rear.

The mounted soldiers made a fine sight as they rode away from the town, their helmets and breastplates gleaming, and their scabbards bouncing against their sides. I rode between the two troopers who had been ordered to look after me; no doubt they were there not only to protect me, but also to see that if there were any treachery I did not escape.

We rode up to the ridge, not hurrying as we were in plenty of time. As we came over the summit, past the ashes of my signal fire, I tried to imagine what might be happening in the towns faintly seen in the distance, what sudden attacks and desperate struggles, Englishmen fighting each other, and some of them no doubt already lying dead in the streets. I could not help being anxious that the rising might have failed, and even now Mr Webb and his fellows could be dead or in chains, and the enemy alerted to our coming. We might indeed be riding into a trap.

But as we drew nearer the town, and with a mile or so more to go, and still had not seen any sign of the Cavaliers (or indeed of the Roundhead plotters), I began to wonder whether the rising had been attempted at all. Supposing Mr Webb had failed to see my signal, or been unable to muster his forces, and the Cavaliers were ignorant of our approach—what would happen? Would there be a sharp fight? Would we perhaps have to withdraw until Lord Essex's main army could come over the ridge? If it came to a siege he might withdraw altogether. He would be in great trouble with Parliament, and might even be dismissed in disgrace—and then what would happen to our Cause, with the Cavaliers triumphant?

We reached the place where the sentry post had been and passed the barricade. There was no one about, but a musket lay at the side of the road half hidden in the grass, and a soldier's helmet had been abandoned nearby. Then we saw the body of a soldier lying in the ditch. He had been shot through the head. It certainly looked as if there had been some sort of skirmish here. Then, a little further on, we met a man waving the flag of Parliament. It was none other than Obadiah Horner. He called out to Lord Essex, 'Welcome, my lord! Take possession of the town of Melcombe!'

'Is the town safe?' asked the Earl.

'It is, sir, Melcombe is yours. But come speedily to the bridge, for the enemy still hold the castle and may try to counter-attack.'

It was not until afterwards, of course, that I heard what had occurred. In fact it was not until about a week later when I happened to meet Obadiah Horner in Dorchester and I heard his account that I could fit everything together. But my story will be clearer if I insert here what he told me.

We saw the smoke from your signal fire rising from the ridge on Saturday evening (said Mr Horner). One of Mr Webb's bodyguards, the big fellows he calls Gog and Magog, saw it first, and came in at once to tell us. We had alerted our leading men to be ready, but did not call them together before we had definite news in case the garrison got wind of what was afoot. Before we had your signal we suspected the Cavaliers knew of Lord Essex moving to Dorset, for we could see that there was unusual activity amongst them. They doubled the guards at Chapel Fort and send a dozen or so soldiers to man the check-point on the Dorchester road.

Mr Webb was in a high state of excitement, because he thought there had surely been time for Lord Essex to reach Dorchester, and he was very anxious if possible to start our rising (for the reasons he told you) on the Lord's Day. He was pacing up and down, and kept sending out to the guards to ask whether they could see anything.

'All is in readiness,' he exclaimed more than once. 'If we do not strike now I fear we shall never do it. And the longer we wait the more dangerous it will be, for there is always the danger that someone may betray us.'

You can imagine our relief when Ted—Gog—came in at last and said he had seen the smoke. We rushed to an upper window to see for ourselves, and then Webb sent a couple of servants out to call the rest of our leading people together, and within little more than an hour we were all assembled.

Mr Webb had already made careful plans with details of who

would go to different points, and what each had to do, and had tried to anticipate what might happen. For example, he had made alternative plans for what to do if the initial assault on Chapel Fort were unsuccessful, and if we should have to pull up the drawbridge and leave the Weymouth side in the enemy's control.

When we were all gathered he addressed us:

'The moment we've been planning for and waiting for has come at last. We have had the signal that tells us Lord Essex is in Dorchester and will be on his way here tomorrow. Each of you has his own work to do, which you already know. If we all work together we shall surely prevail and win a famous victory. All I have to do now is arrange with you the time we shall begin, and deal with any difficulties which may have arisen since our last meeting.'

'There is one problem,' said John Turner, whose task it was to clear the Dorchester road. 'The Cavaliers have sent soldiers to man the block-house on the way to Radipole, but not just a couple of sentries as before. I saw at least a dozen, if not more, going to mount guard there. It is clear that they are aware of of the Earl's approach, and I fear they'll not be easy to surprise or overcome.'

There was a murmur of agreement from the company.

'We have lost the chance of taking them unawares,' said one. 'If indeed they have news of Essex being near, they'll be thoroughly on their guard.'

But Mr Webb was not daunted.

'They have no doubt heard in general that there is an army in Dorset, and may even know that Lord Essex has reached Dorchester. But they won't know that he aims to come here, especially as Lyme is at this moment in desperate need of being relieved. So I still maintain that we can surprise them. We shall start our attack at just before dawn tomorrow. The signal will be the ringing of the Melcombe church bell. Before that you must have your men in position, and as soon as you hear the sound, go into the attack.

'As for your problem of a bigger force than you expected

towards Radipole, Mr Turner, remember that they won't all be awake and alert. You'll probably catch more than half of them bedded down in the block-house. Press home your first assault with vigour and I warrant you they'll run! And that applies to everyone,' he added. 'We must make them panic as they're roused from sleep, and cause them to think a whole army is upon them. Remember Gideon, and how with three hundred he frightened the hordes of Midian and put them to flight.'

'There's another difficulty,' said Zacharias Finn, whose task it was to go furthest along the Preston road to the east and attack the Mountjoy Fort. 'Because the enemy seem worried, they've stepped up the night patrols in the streets. We may find it harder to get our men into position to launch the attack without being seen.'

'I know it,' said Webb, 'but they can't be everywhere at once, and I am confident that you will be able to avoid them. You'll just have to impress on your men to be more careful, and not to make any noise. But one thing is certain, we must all be ready to launch our attacks at the same moment, as soon as we hear the bell.'

There was a little more discussion and making final arrangements, until at last Mr Webb dismissed them:

'Now, to your places! and may Lord prosper the work we are about to do, and bring us to a happy conclusion.'

So off the officers went to their various areas and began to gather their men. As Mr Webb's assistant I mostly kept close to him, but he sent me on a number of errands, and I brought him back news of how the arrangements were going.

During the night small groups of our people walked warily through the dark streets to their appointed places, ready to dodge into the shadows if a Cavalier patrol came their way. Many were armed with swords and pistols which they had retrieved from the hiding places where they had put them when Prince Maurice captured our towns last year.

Some had other weapons which they had improvised or made themselves: knives, bill-hooks, clubs, and some bombs or petards made with gunpowder. A few weeks before we had managed to steal a barrel of powder from under the noses of the sentries on the quay, and had been secretly using it to make bombs. These were probably as dangerous to us as to the Cavaliers, and we were lucky that none of us were blown up prematurely, but we thought it worth taking the risk because they made a great flash and noise, and we hoped that they would spread panic amongst the enemy.

Our main forces were concentrated to attack two key places: Chapel Fort in Weymouth and the drawbridge that joins Weymouth to Melcombe. Mr Webb had also posted a few men with muskets near Sandsfoot Castle, whose task it would be to dissuade the garrison there from coming to the aid of their comrades in the town.

I can tell you my heart was beating so hard I feared the Cavaliers would hear it as the night drew on towards dawn. At last the moment came, and Mr Webb sent me to ring the bell.

The church was still in darkness, and I had to feel my way to the bell-rope. I took the end of the rope, the sally, and thought, I am about to send I know not how many men to their deaths, maybe myself as well! But I grasped the sally more firmly, shut my eyes and pulled. The bell sang out above me, and almost at once there were bangs and cracks of musket-shots and louder booms as our home-made petards exploded.

After ringing the bell for a minute or two, and fearing every moment that Cavaliers would rush in to stop me, I stumbled out of the church and made my way towards the bridge, where I hoped to find Mr Webb.

But when I reached the bridge it had already been taken, because the Cavaliers had only had a couple of sentries posted there, and they were easily overpowered. Behind me somewhere in Melcombe there was an enemy patrol and there were also some soldiers and Royalist sailors by the harbour. So I hurried on across the bridge towards Chapel Fort.

As you will know, this is on the high ground above the river and harbour, and might have beaten off our attack. But it seems that although the enemy knew the Roundheads were in Dorchester, and thought an assault might come along the road from there, they had no idea that we would attack them in the centre of Weymouth.

We had given much thought as to how we could take the Fort, and had been able to place one of our people inside it. He had been taken on as a servant to sweep the floors, wash dishes and fetch firewood, and had pretended to support the Royalist cause. In fact he was a staunch Parliament man, and a very brave one, for he crept down before dawn, stepped over the sleeping sentry, slid back the heavy beam that secured the door and crept back to the kitchen quarters shortly before the bell began to toll.

Our people had the advantage of complete surprise. They mounted a diversionary attack on the other side of the Fort, and a minute or two later, when the garrison's attention had been drawn to that side, assaulted the door. There was a tremendous bang as one of our home-made bombs exploded, the door was battered open and our people rushed in. One of them received a pistol shot in his shoulder, but the Cavaliers panicked and surrendered almost at once.

At the Dorchester road barricade our men also had a quick victory. The sentries were looking in the Dorchester direction and not expecting an attack from their rear, and most of the other soldiers there were asleep in a house they had commandeered. The attackers came on with blood-curdling yells and shot the sentries before they could recover from their surprise.

The other soldiers came pouring out of the house in confusion, some of them with their britches untied and without boots on. Several were clubbed, a couple got away, and the rest surrendered. The two who ran away were found later cowering behind a wall, and joined the other captives.

I heard all about that later. I had reached Chapel Fort just as its last resistance ended, and there I found Mr Webb. He was, as you can imagine, full of joy at winning the Fort so quickly and without loss to our people.

But now we heard shouts and some shots from below in the

direction of the harbour, and men came running along below the Fort and began to climb the hill. We let fly a few shots at them, and they soon realised that the Fort was in our hands, so most of them ran on out of range and escaped to Sandsfoot Castle. The men Mr Webb had posted there wisely let them pass, for they were well armed and might have done mischief, whereas in the Castle they could be kept bottled up close until Lord Essex arrived.

The garrison in the Castle had heard the noises of battle of course, but when some of them issued forth our men shot at them, so that (probably thinking they were being attacked by a large force) they retreated inside the Castle again. Then when their comrades from the harbour ran up, saying that the Roundheads were upon them, they barred the gate and no doubt manned the guns and awaited an attack, but did not attempt to come out.

Meanwhile I went with Mr Webb as he led a party down to the harbour to try to capture the Royalist ship that was there. But we were too late, for when they had heard the shouts and noise of fighting the sailors got quickly aboard and stood out away from the quay. However, they didn't get far, for they dared not put right out to sea because the Earl of Warwick had a squadron of Parliament's ships, which had been supplying our besieged brethren at Lyme, and were thought to be somewhere in the bay.

We then turned back and went across the bridge to Melcombe to deal with the remaining enemy over there. As I mentioned, some of the Cavaliers were patrolling the streets, and although they were few in number (there were only ten or a dozen) they caused more trouble than all the rest. This was because when they heard the noise they did not panic, but took stock of the situation and hid among the houses. They came on with great care, and might have done serious damage, especially when they drew near to the bridge.

The first we knew of them coming was a sudden volley of shots flying into our midst. It was a miracle that only one of our men was killed—a musket ball through his chest. Several more were wounded, and it was touch and go whether we would stand or run.

It was all too clear that the enemy would try to recapture the bridge and, with their swords and muskets, could kill or maim many of us, for remember we weren't trained soldiers, most of us.

While things were looking so black, and the success of our rising was being put in doubt by these few enemy soldiers, help came from those who had overcome the Dorchester road barricade. They were now armed with weapons they had captured, and coming upon the soldiers of the patrol from behind they directed musket and pistol shots at their rear.

As a result the Cavaliers lost heart and, probably also thinking that the forces against them were larger than they really were, surrendered. As with their comrades from the barricade and the Fort, we took their weapons and made them sit on the ground with their ankles hobbled, guarded by some of our men with pistols.

Mr Webb then sent others of his men around both towns proclaiming their new allegiance to Parliament, and warning the townspeople to stay indoors until Lord Essex should arrive. Like you in Dorchester and in many other places in Dorset, Melcombe and Weymouth are very divided, and we knew that not everybody would welcome the change of allegiance, so Mr Webb was determined not to allow possible objectors to assemble until the change-over was secure. He also sent men to the harbour to prevent the Royalist sailors from coming back to the quay and causing trouble. And myself he sent with all speed to meet Lord Essex with a Parliament flag and try to hurry his advance. But that you know, for I saw you with him.

So much for Obadiah Horner's story; I will now continue with what I saw myself. As soon as he heard Mr Horner's call for help Lord Essex shouted to Sir William Balfour to order the troops to canter. As we rode through the town a few people who had ignored the instructions to stay indoors stood by and two or three cheered, but we did not stop until we came to the drawbridge which leads across to Weymouth. There I saw Mr Webb waving a sword in one hand and the Parliament colours in the other. He too called out a welcome.

'We have taken the town and the fort,' he cried. 'All is yours, my lord. Pray take possession in the name of Parliament.'

'Well done, excellently done!' said Essex. He leant from his horse to speak quietly with Mr Webb, then spoke to a captain who then called out to his men:

'Come on, lads. The bulk of the enemy are up in the Castle, and we're going to see that they don't get out. Follow me!' They clattered over the bridge and were soon out of sight.

Quite a lot of the townsfolk were now gathering, and Essex addressed them:

'Good people of Weymouth and Melcombe, you have been delivered, by your own efforts, from the tyranny of the Cavaliers. My men have orders to behave as befits soldiers of Christ and of Parliament. We will not be with you to oppress you with a long stay. As soon as we have captured the Castle we shall go on to sweep the enemy from the whole of the west country. On, then, to victory—and if any of you men would care to join us you will be most welcome, and will go with us on the path to glory.'

A number of the townsfolk pressed forward to congratulate him, and his officers, no doubt fearing treachery, crowded about to protect him. There were people shouting and singing and dancing in the street. Some waved Parliament flags, others just waved their arms in the air and cheered. Everyone, it seemed, had all along been a Roundhead and had hated being ruled by the Cavaliers!

Lord Essex now drew aside to confer with his staff, and I seized the chance of approaching Mr Webb, who was accompanied (I was sorry to see) by his two brutal-looking henchmen. Dismounting near him I pushed forward leading my horse.

'Sir,' I said, 'may I congratulate you. You have indeed done wonders against the enemy!'

He turned and gave me a tight-lipped smile.

'Mr Judd! I am glad you have witnessed this day,' he said. 'Yes, sir, all has gone as planned so far, though at the last it was a close run thing, and I thank you for your part in it. We could not have had so much support in the town if the Earl himself had not come.'

'You owe me a favour then,' I said.

His smile vanished.

'What is it you want?' he demanded.

'The truth—the truth about George Godwin, I mean.'

'What about him?' he said, and the bodyguards drew closer.

'Who killed him? When I met you first you implied that you had somehow been behind his death.'

'It is no business of yours whether I was or not.' He began to turn away, and I caught his arm. The bodyguards came on each side of me, and one seized my horse's bridle.

'Mr Webb, I have done you good service and you must not brush me aside. A man lies in Dorchester gaol accused of Godwin's murder, and if he is innocent he must be cleared. So in God's name tell me, did you have a hand in Godwin's death?'

He turned back and looked me straight in the eye.

'I did not,' he said. 'I had trusted him fully, used him as our messenger to Dorchester and in other ways, let him be nominal leader of our band and party to all our plans, and then I found that some of them were becoming known to the enemy. I began to suspect him of treachery, of playing a double game with that cousin of his, Sir James. I had resolved to take action against him, so I welcomed his death, which saved me the trouble. But I did not kill him.'

'Did you have proof of his treachery?'

'No. I was intending to question him, with the help of Gog and Magog—' He gave his thin smile for a moment '—on the very day he died. Perhaps you should examine Sir James about it. A double-agent is in danger from both sides.'

'I will do so if I can find him.'

'Is he not the man in gaol in Dorchester?'

'No, sir, the prisoner is a poor old man from Upwey who is

likely to take the blame.'

'Then you should go and look for Sir James, for you have my word that I did not kill Godwin, though who knows what I might have done had he not died when he did.'

'I believe you,' I said, 'for I think there is no reason for you to deceive me. Thank you, Mr Webb.'

'Come,' he said to his henchmen, and they let go of me and moved off with him.

I looked about and saw where Lord Essex was still conferring with his officers. I led my horse in his direction, but was prevented from approaching by soldiers. So I mounted in order to be more visible, and rode round to where he could see me. When he had finished giving some orders, and various officers and messengers had ridden away and the Earl himself seemed about to leave, I seized the moment and waved my hat in the air and shouted, 'God save you, my lord!' and caught his eye. He signed to the soldiers to let me through.

'Well done, Mr Judd,' he said, 'you were a true messenger. I don't mind confessing that I had my doubts about this business. But all has gone well, and I thank you.'

'May I make a request, my lord,' I said. 'There is a very malignant Royalist who nearly brought this whole enterprise to ruin. It is suspected that he murdered one of the Parliament men here. Please may he be arrested and questioned about what he has done.'

'Who is this man?' asked the Earl.

'His name is Sir James Freke, and he lives at Upwey, between here and Dorchester.'

'Then by all means arrest him. You can have some of my men to help. Sergeant,' he ordered, 'send four men with Mr Judd to arrest this man. You had better bring him back to me here.'

He rode off with his staff into Weymouth town, and the sergeant, after asking me how long we would be, told four of his men to go with me. We rode back the way we had come, and as we went along near the sea I noticed that some ships out in the bay were flying the Parliament flag. They must have been part of the Earl of Warwick's squadron which had been supplying the besieged people of Lyme. I believe soon after I saw them they captured the Royalist ship when it tried to slip out of the harbour.

As we rode out along the Dorchester road we saw the rest of Essex's army was coming down over the ridge and streaming towards Melcombe. At times we had to draw off the road to get by. My companions had to put up with quite a lot of good-natured banter.

'Oi, Johnny boy,' one called out, 'you lost your way?'

'You're going the wrong way!' said another.

'Forgotten yer dinner? Left it behind in Dorchester?'

'Nah, it's not his dinner, it's his girl!'

At last we turned aside towards Upwey, came to Sir James's mansion and rode up to the door. I dismounted and knocked, and eventually a serving-man opened it.

'We have come to see Sir James Freke,' I said.

'He is not here.'

'Where is he?'

'I do not know. He has gone to fight for the King.'

'What do you mean?'

'He heard that an army of Roundheads was coming, and he said—I heard him myself—"I've sat aside for too long. I must go and do my part". And he got his things together and rode off early this morning.'

'Where was he going?'

'I don't know, sir. He did not say.'

There seemed nothing for it but to leave, for the bird had flown. I turned to thank the troopers and dismiss them. But then I saw Sir James's groom, the fellow I had met outside the cottage where Mr Godwin had died.

'Hey man,' I called, 'did you saddle Sir James's horse this

morning?'

'I did, sir.'

'Where was he going?'

'Wareham, I believe. He said he was going to join Colonel O'Brien, who is at Wareham, I think.'

That seemed a likely destination. With Dorchester in Roundhead hands the road to Sherborne would be blocked, and Wareham was the next best place for a would-be Cavalier soldier to make for.

So I parted from the troopers, who rode off back towards Melcombe, while I took my way over the ridge and home. I was glad to have seen the success of the Roundheads in Weymouth, but sad that Sir James had escaped me. My chances of saving Malachy now seemed even smaller, and I did not know how he could be helped.

For the next week or two I concentrated on my proper work, and on continuing to instruct Matthew Barton in apothecary's work. He asked many questions, but I was glad to answer them as well as I could, for he was so eager to learn, and was soon able to help me in numerous ways, preparing medicines from herbs and wild plants, minding the shop when I was out, and taking packages to various folk about the town. I still attended to people in outlying parts, for which work I found my horse very useful.

There was much for me to do. Although Essex's troops had passed on, and he did not even leave a garrison in Dorchester, they left an unpleasant reminder of their passing. Several of the townsfolk were very ill with a fever brought by the soldiers. Those who caught it were horribly sick, frequently vomiting and purging and becoming feverish and weak. In spite of all I and the physicians could do, several died. I gave them a decoction of St John's wort with juices of knot-grass, which helped some, and eventually the sickness worked itself out.

One day I met Obadiah Horner in the High Street. He had been to see Mr Barton, I believe. I invited him to my shop and he told me the story of the Roundhead rising in Melcombe as I recounted earlier. He also brought news that Sandsfoot Castle had surrendered, (which left only Portland Castle in Royalist hands), and that the Earl of Essex had moved on. He had left a garrison to hold Weymouth for Parliament, though Mr Horner was worried that it was too small.

Soon after that we heard that Prince Maurice had raised the siege of Lyme when he heard Essex was coming, and we really began to think that the war might be over in our part of the country and that the Cavaliers were now really on the run. We could not have been more wrong!

Lord Essex led his army along the coast to Bridport, then north to Crewkerne and Chard, leaving sickness in his wake. In spite of that he was joined by many volunteers. He recruited over three hundred from Weymouth alone, and was everywhere greeted joyfully as the victor. On the whole his troops did behave better than the Cavaliers had done. He was certainly a more humane general than Prince Maurice. But he delayed too long, I think, and when he eventually headed for the far west he went to a humiliating and disastrous defeat. Also he did not do a thorough enough job in our part. Besides Portland Castle, he left Wareham, Corfe and Sherborne in Royalist hands, and did not even capture the Strangways little stronghold at Abbotsbury as he went by. All these spelt trouble for the future, and I was not alone in beginning to feel that all our efforts might have been in vain. It would be all too easy for Lord Hopton or Colonel O'Brien to come roaring out from Sherborne or Wareham, as soon as Essex was well out of the way, and capture the county for the King again. Was it worth risking our lives for a Cause that seemed to be so badly managed?

But now I had more pressing personal worries, for I was in danger of being accused of having dealings with the devil.

Chapter 12 Satanic influences?

IT WAS OF COURSE because of my association with Malachy. Some of the odour of Satan which hung about him was beginning to cling to me—at least in the noses of some.

Having acquired a few bottles of French wine from my disreputable friend Jacob Perrin, I met his brother-in-law, Lawrence Huatt the pewterer, in the market and invited him to come home with me for a glass. To my surprise he appeared embarrassed.

'Excuse me, Mr Judd, I really can't spare the time today. I... I must get back to my workshop. Thank you, thank you,' and he hurried away. Yet a little later I caught sight of him still in the market and talking to another old acquaintance. When he saw me Huatt turned, said something to his companion and hurried away.

Then an old customer of mine, a Mrs Ainsley, who used to come regularly every Wednesday to buy a cordial of motherwort to take melancholy vapours from her heart, failed to call. I saw her later in the town and asked her if all was well. She appeared a little awkward.

'Mr Judd, I'm sorry,' she said. 'I don't think I'll be wanting more of your cordial. I'll manage without it. 'Twas but a luxury which I don't really need. Thank you, Mr Judd.' And before I could reply she too hurried away.

When I went to collect my new doublet and breeches from Tom Hartley I asked him what was the matter with folk.

'Is something wrong?' I asked him. 'People seem to be avoiding me and my shop.'

'You know why,' he said, 'they're frightened, I guess.'

'Frightened? whatever of?'

'Of the devil, I suppose. They think you're associating with Old

Nick, and are afraid that some of his dark influences may attach to them if they see too much o' you. I did warn you it might happen.'

'But that's ridiculous,' I said. Even if old Malachy is in league with the devil, which I don't for a moment believe, he's not bewitched me. I'm surely known as a good church-going Christian.'

'Makes no difference,' said Tom. 'They're think some tincture of Satan may have rubbed off on you, and might get passed to them. It's like the plague.'

'The devil it is,' I said. 'Well, I'm not going to abandon that poor old man just because a few blunder-headed folk get silly ideas. You don't believe this nonsense, do you, Tom?'

'Noo,' he said doubtfully, 'but then I know you pretty well, and they may not. But take care, Micah, for there are a lot of people in this town who believe your Mr Moore is a wizard or he-witch, and are really and truly afraid o' the devil's power. An' some o' them also think apothecaries are a sight too familiar with Satan and get their cures from the powers o' darkness. So if I were you I'd take great care not to give 'em grounds for suspecting it!'

I made an angry exclamation, but thanked him for his advice as well as his workmanship as I took the clothes. I'm sometimes obstinate, I know, and I determined not to be swayed by the attitudes of ignorant people. Yet I was worried, for I did not want my business or my family to suffer because of my stand.

And soon I had even greater worry and sadness made worse by my association with Malachy.

It was on a Friday that Agnes began to feel pains, although her time was not due for another fortnight. But we remembered that our firstborn, Mark, had arrived early, so as her pains continued I sent Hester to fetch the midwife.

Mrs Thornlow was very experienced, and had, I suppose, helped to bring half the town into the world. She was a short stout woman with straight black hair streaked with grey and a somewhat ugly pock-marked face and a wide red nose. But she had a reassuring confident manner, and I felt happier when she arrived.

She at once turned me out of the bedroom, sending me to ask Hester for towels and warm water from the kitchen. When I had done that I tried to attend to my business, occupying myself in the shop, making up medicines and serving the few people who called in. I also prepared a decoction of avens or herb bennet in the hope that it might help Agnes. But when I took it upstairs Mrs Thornlow just took it and shut the door on me again, saying, 'You can't do any good in here, sir. You'd do better to take you to your prayers.'

I wrote a note to Agnes's parents in Fordington to tell them that her time seemed to have come early, and sent it by Andy, a boy from up the lane who often runs errands for me.

But as the day wore on and there was no sign of them, and no word from the bedroom, at last I insisted on going in. Agnes was lying on the bed looking very pale and groaning every now and then. She tossed and turned and then cried, 'Oh!' and I thought the birth was imminent. But then she sank back and was still, though breathing heavily.

'Do you think I had better send for a physician?' I asked the midwife, but she shook her head.

'There's nothing your dear wife needs but a good push when the moment comes,' she said. 'Come on, my dearie, next time you must push harder.'

But after another hour I could stand it no longer. I wrote another urgent note to Agnes's parents to come at once, and Joel Andrews kindly agreed to send his maidservant with it.

'I am going to get Doctor Losse,' I told the midwife, and went myself to fetch him.

Doctor Frederick Losse was a distinguished physician from Germany, a graduate of Heidelburg, who had come to England to escape from the wars which had devastated his homeland. He had settled in Dorchester, and was a good friend and supporter of our famous minister, the Reverend John White. Although Doctor Losse was now quite old I felt sure that if I could persuade him to come there would be a good chance of saving both mother and child. I was worried though, because so many wives die in what the Prayer Book calls 'the great pain and peril of childbirth'. Because of my work I probably know more than most men about the risks women face in giving birth.

Fortunately I found the good doctor at home, and he agreed to come at once.

'I must just fetch my instruments,' he said. Every physician has his own favourite instruments to help with difficult births, often devised by himself and kept a closely guarded secret from his fellows. Doctor Losse's were in a leather case which he would not let me carry for him.

Back at my house he went straight upstairs to Agnes and felt her pulse, then ran his hands over her belly.

'How long has she been like this?' he asked Mrs Thornlow, who had drawn aside to the window, not (I think) liking his involvement.

'It was late morning when I was called,' she said. 'I've been waiting since then for her to give a proper push.'

'She needs more than that,' said the doctor, opening his bag. In it I saw he had various instruments of iron with wooden handles, some like hooks or spirals, one like a large spoon.

I cannot describe in detail what happened during the next hour. I was too distressed and worried, and am even now confused as to exactly what occurred. I know Doctor Losse was on one side of the bed and Mrs Thornlow on the other, while I held Agnes's hand and Hester went to and fro with water and towels and whatever else the doctor called for. In the middle of all this Agnes's parents arrived full of anxiety. They had been out in the morning, and only after Joel's maid came had they found my first note, which the boy had pushed under their door. They came and knelt by the bed.

Agnes groaned and cried and perspired. The doctor used one, or maybe two, of his instruments, and he too perspired freely with the effort. But at last he drew out a small, very small, girl babe, and after tying and cutting the cord he handed her to Mrs Thornlow, who smacked the infant to make it cry.

After the effort of giving birth Agnes lay back on the bed so still that I feared she was dead. But when I squeezed her hand she opened her eyes for a moment.

'I think we had better christen this little mite, she's so small,' said Mrs Thornlow. 'Shall I do it, sir? You can have it done proper like in church if she lives.'

'Yes, please do,' I said.

'Have you thought of a name for her?'

'Yes, we agreed if it was a girl to call her Thomasyn after my late mother.'

Mrs Thornlow went to where Hester was holding a bowl of water.

'I baptise thee, Thomasyn, in the name of the Father, Son and Holy Ghost,' she said, sprinkling some water on the baby's head. 'There now, whatever happens she'll be among the blessed ones.'

I turned back to Agnes. She was dreadfully pale, hovering between life and death. Little Mark crept into the room and I held him in my arms. Doctor Losse felt her wrist. Some minutes went by.

'Doctor,' said Mrs Thornlow in an urgent voice. He turned to where she was holding the tiny baby wrapped in a shawl.

'I think she's gone,' she said.

Doctor Losse touched the little head, then took the babe from her. He bent over the child, then said, 'I'm afraid so, her soul has fled.'

He laid down the little body and turned back to Agnes. For what seemed an age we were there, watching, unable to do anything except wait—and hope.

At last Agnes seemed to breathe more easily and regularly and to sink into a quiet sleep. The doctor and midwife left, Doctor Losse telling me to call him at once if Agnes had any turn for the worse.

'But now I think she will recover,' he said, 'unless she develops fever. But she is young and strong, and should live to bear more children, I hope.'

Her parents stayed with her while I saw the doctor out and made sure that Hester was looking after Mark.

It was later, when the parents, Mr and Mrs Goddin, came down, that Agnes's mother said a thing that pierced my heart.

'This is what comes of consorting with the devil.'

'What do you mean?' I demanded, though I knew too well what she was referring to.

'It's that he-witch in the gaol,' she said. 'It's well known that you go to him; and now see what sadness it has brought upon the family—the little babe dead and our darling Agnes at death's door. How can you bear to have done it?'

'But this is nonsense, it's utterly wrong,' I retorted. 'Have you so little faith in God that you think the devil can overcome Him? Didn't you lose babies? You had six, I know, and only Agnes survived to grow up. You're not going to say that you lost the others because you were consorting with the devil. What rubbish!'

I spoke heatedly because I was very upset both by Agnes's sickness, the babe's death, and now by the hateful suggestion that was being put to me. If Agnes's parents thought like that, what might my fellow townsmen be saying about me? But my heat offended Mrs Goddin.

'That is a very hurtful thing to say, Micah,' she said.

'Well, please don't suggest it to me, mother,' I said. 'We both know how often babies and children die. I know a family where they've had thirteen children, and all were dead before the age of five. So don't let's quarrel, specially not now when we're overwrought.'

'No,' said Agnes's father, 'we must support each other, and pray God that Agnes may come through.'

She did recover remarkably quickly, though we were both very sad to have lost our little daughter. On the next Tuesday I took the tiny coffin for her to be buried in St Peter's churchyard. Agnes was not well enough to come, but her parents were there, and the minister said a few prayers very feelingly. It was such a small grave, yet little Thomasyn had been perfectly formed and would have grown into a lovely woman had she lived.

Agnes's mother said no more about the evil influence of Malachy upon our family, in fact she apologised.

'I ought not to have said what I did the other day, Micah. I was overwrought, and so worried about dear Agnes.'

But she could not blot out what she had said, and I suspected she still thought it in her heart. And she was not the only one to draw conclusions from our little tragedy. People who should have known better said things like, 'What can you expect when Mr Judd consorts with the devil?' and, 'My heart bleeds for that Agnes Judd, being married to a man who dabbles with Satan.' I seriously wondered whether I ought for all our sakes to cease supporting Malachy.

While I was turning this over in my mind I happened to meet Rachel Haggard in the street. She looked so bright and sweet that I thought, 'She's been seeing that old fellow, even touching him and taking his dirty clothes to wash, yet she looks more radiant than ever. He surely can't have an evil influence!'

So I stopped and asked her if she was still visiting him.

'Oh yes,' she said, 'I go there every day or two if I can. He's such an interesting old man. He knows a lot about birds and wild creatures, and he talks about his cat, Simmany, who was so clever. He loved Simmany more than anyone, I think.'

'He must talk much more to you than he does to me,' I said. 'I find it hard to get a word out of him.'

'Oh, he talks enough to me. He calls me his angel, and chatters away. I love to hear him talk.'

'Tell me,' I said, 'people are saying I'm consorting with the devil, and other horrid remarks, and some are avoiding me because I've been to see Malachy. Do they do the same to you?'

'I haven't noticed it,' she replied. 'One or two have said silly things, but I pay no heed to them. They're not people I want to know anyway.'

'Do you think Malachy is in league with Satan, or dabbles in evil?'

'Of course not,' she said. 'People say all sorts of unkind things sometimes—the gaol-keeper for one, he's a silly surly fellow, isn't he? But old Malachy reminds me of my granddad who died when I was small. He shouldn't be in prison at all.'

'Then you don't think I'm wrong to be associated with him?'

'Oh no, Mr Judd,' she said seriously, 'your support is very important to him. Do remember what you told me when I first met you, "Things come around". I'm sure they will, so please don't even think of giving him up.'

What could I do in the face of such loyalty? I felt encouraged by her firmness, and my admiration for her increased. Matthew would be a lucky fellow if he could marry her!

When Agnes was well enough she went with Mark to stay with her parents in Fordington for a time, to get away from our house while the loss of Thomasyn was so fresh, and to be pampered for a space until she was quite recovered.

I busied myself in my work and in teaching Matthew more about herbs and their use in medicines. I did not go into the deeper parts of astrology, and the influence of the heavenly bodies, though I told him that if he wished to go on in the work he would need to study such things. But the straightforward use of herbs, and which were moist and cooling, which heating and fiery, and other such plain knowledge I did impart, and found him very ready to learn.

I also talked to him about Malachy and Rachel's involvement with the old man.

'Her father is quite angry with her, and has tried to dissuade her from visiting the prison,' Matthew told me.

'So what will she do?'

'She'll take no notice, I'm sure. Her father is really very fond of her, and would do almost anything she wanted—except agreeing for her to marry me.'

Then a day or two later Matthew told me his father had also been speaking of Malachy.

'Father was talking to Sir Richard Strode yesterday,' he said. 'Apparently they're going to try to get some of the justices together to hold a court. The war and the fact that so many of the justices have become involved on opposing sides has made it difficult to deal with lawbreakers, and nobody's sure whether the judges will be able to come on circuit. So Sir Richard was hoping they could deal with what he called 'that old he-witch' themselves very soon.'

'Do you know when the trial will be?' I asked.

'Father said he thought it would be in the second week of July.'

'Does your father assume that Malachy's guilty?'

'I'm afraid so. In fact he told me I was a fool to keep coming to work for you. He's in a bit of a quandary, because he thinks you did a lot of good in the Weymouth affair, and getting Lord Essex to come. But he's afraid some evil influence will rub off onto me. I told him he was quite mistaken (I said it respectfully!), and he hasn't absolutely forbidden me to come. But if the magistrates share his attitude I wouldn't give much for Malachy's chances.'

As the day of the trial drew near Matthew's fears seemed all too likely to be fulfilled.

Chapter 13 Witch-trial

I HEARD THAT the justices were going to hold court in Dorchester itself, which was not usually on their peace-time circuit. They were to sit in a large room at the Antelope Inn. Murder and witchcraft would normally have been kept for the judges' Assizes, but what Matthew had heard proved right—that because of the disturbed times the magistrates had decided that they would hear this case. However, until shortly before the trial it was doubtful which of them would be able to attend.

I went to see Malachy at the beginning of July, the gaol-keeper greeted me with, 'Your friend the he-witch has got company!'

'Visitors, do you mean?'

'Nah, prisoners—three thieves and a man from Tolpuddle who's been sticking his trowel into his neighbour's garden.'

'Stealing cabbages?'

'Nah, stealing his neighbour's wife. More 'n that, he's been beating up his own wife worse than a husband ought to do.'

He let me through the inner door and bolted it behind me, and I took in the scene.

There were the three, presumably the thieves, sitting together, a thoroughly ruffianly looking lot, and cheerful but very dirty. There was the wife-beater, looking like a respectable smith or shepherd, sitting a little apart with his arms folded, looking glum. And on the other side of the room, avoided as far as possible by the others, was Malachy. I thought he was looking thinner than before, but still clean and with more colour in his cheeks.

'I'm sorry not to have been to see you lately,' I said. 'I had family trouble which prevented me. But I hope you have had proper food and not been ill-treated.'

He looked at me with his sad eyes and paused before answering:

''Ees, thank 'ee, zur. My angel has been to see me. I can't complain.'

'Your angel—the young maiden—has she been often?'

'She has, zur, an' brought me clean clothes an' a bite to eat. Every second day she's been, zur, straight from heaven, she be.'

'I'm very glad of that,' I said, sitting down beside him. 'But now we must think about your trial. It's coming up next week. You ought to have a lawyer to advise you.'

'No zur, no lawyers. I bain't having no lawyers.'

'But if you're found guilty you'll be condemned.'

'There's no help for it, zur. They won't let me live, whatever you mid say for me.'

'Have you thought how you'll plead, or what you'll say?'

'No zur, there's no use in saying aught.'

'But if they say you killed Mr Godwin, you can surely say, "Not guilty"!'

'But I did kill 'un. I don't know that I really meant to. But I cussed him an' hc died.'

'How many times have I got to tell you that your curses had nothing to do with it. He was killed by someone who thought him a traitor—I'm certain of it.'

'I know nothin' o' that. All I know is, I cussed him an' he died.'

'Well, don't admit it,' I said, 'let them try to prove it if they can. You keep quiet about your cursing. But the other thing they'll try to prove is that you're a witch. You don't admit to that, do you? You told me that you had not made any pact with the devil.'

'No zur, I've never had any truck wi' Satan. But I've had powers that many folk say come from him. The parson at home now, he says they come from the devil, and he's called me a chile o' the Evil One many a time.'

'Yes, but you are not to believe him. Don't let them make out you're a witch. Maintain your innocence. When they ask you, you must say "Not guilty".'

''Twill make no difference,' was all he would say. I felt myself getting angry. What could one do for a poor silly old man who wouldn't defend himself? The trouble was that in spite of all I, and no doubt Rachel Haggard, had said to him Malachy was still more than half convinced that his curses had taken effect, and he seemed all too ready to accept what his vicar and neighbours said about him. I was still very afraid that he would plead guilty and admit to anything they might accuse him of.

I suppose I had some self-interest in wanting him to be acquitted, for that would perhaps silence those who were saying such damaging things about me being in league with Satan. But also I wanted justice to be done, and nothing but a 'not guilty' verdict would achieve that.

The trial was fixed for Wednesday, July 10th, and I was sorry to hear that the justices were to be Sir Thomas Trenchard of Wolfeton, Sir Richard Strode of Cattistock, and John Browne Esquire of Frampton. All of them were very experienced, having been on the bench for years, but all three were of Puritan persuasion and therefore, I feared, likely to take a particularly severe view of anything to do with witchcraft. I suppose these three had agreed to sit in Dorchester because they all lived within easy distance and, with Parliament in the ascendant at this time, they were eager to assert their authority in the face of other justices who were Royalists.

Agnes and little Mark came back home on the Sunday before, and I was relieved to see how much better she was, though she still lacked something of her old spirit. Our maid Hester really proved her worth, making Agnes comfortable and encouraging her to take renewed interest in the house and what was going on in the town. In fact the news about Malachy and his coming trial helped to turn Agnes's thoughts outward, away from her own sorrow, for she was as concerned as I was that he should be cleared of wrongdoing.

The day of the trial came at last, and I left Matthew to mind the shop while I made sure I was at the Antelope Inn in good time to have a place. The room was large but soon became crowded and stuffy. I had pressed Nathan Whittle to come, and he had consented, rather against his will, to speak on Malachy's behalf should that be possible, but when I looked around I could not see him.

The three justices took their seats, with Sir Thomas Trenchard as chairman. They all looked severe and rather old, well over sixty I should think, though Sir Richard Strode may have been slightly younger.

Sir Thomas banged on the table in front of them, and the Clerk began to read the Commission in Latin. He stumbled over some of the words and read in a slow monotone, and most of those present paid little attention to him.

He then read out a list of jurors, each of whom said 'Here' or 'Sir' to show they were present. Two names elicited no response, and no doubt these absentees would be fined.

Then came the swearing in of constables, which seemed to go on for an interminable time. In fact all these preliminaries seemed to me to take up far too long. But at last the Clerk turned to Sir Thomas and said 'Sir!'

At this Sir Thomas leant forward and gave his charge to the jurors.

'I have sat as a Justice of the Peace very many times, over twenty, I believe, but never in such troubled times as these. It says much for the great tradition of administering the law in this land of ours than even in such times the machinery of justice can continue to work, and the civil courts to function in spite of the actions of the military.

'Now in this great tradition of justice, which has been passed down to us by our forefathers, you jurymen have a most important part to play. It is for you to hear the evidence, and for you to decide the guilt or otherwise of those who are brought to trial. This is a grave responsibility, the gravest, perhaps, that you will ever be called upon to undertake.

'In view of this I trust you will put from you all prejudice, and thoughts of your own petty concerns and mundane business, and listen with impartial and indifferent ears, and look into these matters with clear and unclouded eyes.'

He went on in this vein for many minutes, and some of the jurymen's eyes looked dull and stupid rather than clear before he had finished. But at last he was done, and I hoped the real business of the day could begin. But no, there were various administrative matters to be settled, appointments to certain annual offices to be made, orders for the repair of a number of roads and bridges to be given, licensing of ale-sellers, and so on.

Then Sir Thomas looked at his watch and announced that the court would adjourn until after dinner.

'We shall reconvene at two o' the clock,' he said, and he and his fellow justices went off to another part of the inn, no doubt to have a hearty meal. I went home feeling rather upset that all these minor matters had taken so long, having been all keyed up for Malachy's trial.

After eating with Agnes, and conferring with Matthew about things in the shop, I went back to the Court Room, which soon filled up again. I was pleased to see that Nathan Whittle had made the effort to be there, and I pushed though the crowd to him.

'I don't think I ought to have come, Micah,' he said. 'I can't swear the old man isn't a witch. In fact I've never seen him before, and only know what you've told me.'

'Don't worry, Nathan,' I said, 'I don't suppose we shall be able to do much before the jury come to their decision. If they do find him guilty we can then put in a plea for mercy. You can say how he saved you from the loss of all your money.'

'I don't like it, Micah, I don't at all. If he is found to be a witch, I don't want it thought that I made use of him. Why, they might accuse me of witchcraft by association!'

I must confess that the same thought had occurred to me. Witchcraft is such a terrible charge, and so difficult to refute, that once a person has been accused of it, even if nothing is proved, some evil odour tends to hang about him for ever after. So Whittle was right that it might be perilous to have had dealings with someone found guilty of witchcraft. It could be dangerous even to speak up for a witch at his trial. I had already experienced the hurts and slanders befriending Malachy could bring, and if he were found guilty my business might be ruined. As Tom Hartley had reminded me, apothecaries are anyway thought by some to associate with devils, to have dangerous knowledge. We use strange remedies, pick herbs when the moon and planets are right, and at times investigate horoscopes. Ignorant people probably think we practise Satanic magic.

But I tried to put such thoughts from me, and firmly told myself that Malachy was a poor old man unjustly accused of murder, and I must stand by him.

At last the justices took their seats again, looking well fed, their faces red and shining, and Sir Thomas nodded to the Clerk of the Peace, who called for Malachy to be fetched. He was led in by the gaol-keeper, and the Clerk read out the charges against him:

'That on Thursday the twenty-third day of May in the year of our Lord 1644 the said Malachy Moore of Upwey being a witch did curse Mr George Godwin so that he died, so that the said Malachy Moore stands accused of murder and witchcraft.'

'Malachy Moore, how do you plead?' asked Sir Thomas.

For a moment I feared that Malachy would say nothing or even plead guilty. He paused so long that Sir Thomas repeated crossly, 'Prisoner, how do you plead?'

Malachy rolled his eyes and licked his lips, and his jaw worked for a moment before the words came out: 'Not guilty, zur.'

The case against the prisoner was then outlined by the court prosecutor, Mr Henry Hynde, a local lawyer. He dwelt much upon what he called 'the prisoner's evil reputation', his cursing, and the horrible death of Mr Godwin. At last he was done, and witnesses were called and sworn.

It turned out that one of Malachy's chief accusers was the vicar of Upwey, the Reverend Jonathan Lawrence, the same clergyman whom I had met at the church there. He testified that over many years he had been concerned about the state of Malachy's soul, that he was often absent from church, and that when he did come he was heard muttering under his breath.

Sir Thomas: What was he muttering?

The minister: Incomprehensible words, sir—spells and incantations, I fear.

Sir Thomas (to Malachy): What were you muttering?

But Malachy said nothing, but merely shook his head from side to side, so Sir Thomas told Mr Lawrence to proceed.

He went on to say how the village people had become afraid of Malachy, and he made much of the way Malachy was seen from time to time, as he put it, 'conjuring with his rod', and that he had a familiar spirit in the form of a black cat, to which he often talked as if it were a person.

Then he came to the events of May 23rd, describing how Malachy had made a 'most terrible and blasphemous curse', which had caused Mr Godwin to fall dead. The vicar described it as if he had witnessed it all, though I was sure he had not.

Sir Thomas asked Malachy if he had anything to say, but he just stared at the ground and shook his head.

Then the woman I had met, in whose cottage Mr Godwin died, told the court what had happened, and the horrid way he had died, and his calling out upon the devil, and how everyone had then rushed off to Malachy's cottage to seize him.

The carter described how the soldiers had prevented the villagers from giving Malachy the water-test for witchcraft, and forced him to carry him to Dorchester.

Through all this Malachy continued to look at the ground and say nothing, though his jaw was working as if he was chewing.

Then Sir Thomas asked, 'Has he been examined for marks of witchcraft on his body?'

'Ay sir,' said the gaol-keeper stepping forward. When he had been duly sworn he testified that he had examined the prisoner in the presence of the minister officiating at All Saints Church at the time, who had since been taken ill, and therefore was unable to be here as a witness. The gaol-keeper greatly feared the minister's illness might be because he had been 'overlooked' by the witch. But he could testify for both of them that they had indeed found devil's nipples on the prisoner, one below the normal nipple on the left side, and one near his fundament on the left buttock.

Sir Thomas: Did you test him in any other way for witchcraft?

Gaol-keeper: Yes, sir, we pricked him with pins, and in several places did not draw blood which, as you know sir, is an infallible sign of the devil.

The final witness was Robert Still, the thief who had been in the prison with Malachy. He testified that he had heard Malachy confess more than once that his curses had killed Mr Godwin, and he added that in the prison Malachy had often prayed to the devil. I was sure this last accusation was a lie.

Sir Richard Strode asked Still why he had been in the prison.

'I was accused of stealing, sir, most unjustly, sir.'

'And were you tried and acquitted?'

'No sir, but for telling what I know in this matter I was let off, sir.'

I longed to be able to question Robert Still to show what a liar he was, but of course, not being a lawyer, I was in no position to do so.

Sir Thomas again asked Malachy whether he had anything to say, and on getting no reply turned to confer with his fellow justices. It seemed to me that, even without being challenged, the evidence against Malachy was very slight, but lacking an advocate or anyone to speak for him, his chances would not be great.

Sir Thomas turned to the jury.

'Well, gentlemen,' he said, 'you have heard the evidence that the prisoner is a witch, and has been such for a number of years, and that on the day in question he did put a curse upon the victim, Mr

Godwin, who then died most horribly in agony. There seems little to add, so I must ask you to consider your verdict.'

I did try to intervene at this point.

'Sir,' I called out, 'is no one to speak on behalf of the prisoner?'

'Who are you, young man?' said Sir Thomas.

'I am a citizen of this town and a friend of the prisoner, sir, and I consider he has been unjustly accused, because the man he is said to have killed was murdered by someone else.'

'Are you a lawyer?'

'No sir, I am an apothecary, and believe Mr Godwin died by poisoning, not witchcraft.'

'If you are not a lawyer you have no right to speak in this court. If the prisoner does not have an advocate and will not speak on his own behalf, there is no more to be said.'

'But this is injustice, sir!'

'Be silent, or I shall have you committed for contempt. Jurymen, you have heard the evidence. Pray consider your verdict.'

They did not take long. They huddled together and talked in low tones with much nodding of heads, and then after less than ten minutes the foreman announced that they were ready.

'And do you find the prisoner guilty or not guilty?'

'Guilty, sir.'

Sir Thomas nodded and conferred again with his fellows. Then, as he seemed about to speak, I tried again to say something on Malachy's behalf.

'Sir,' I said, 'before you pronounce sentence may I testify to the prisoner's character, and make a plea for mercy?'

'Let it not be said that we have denied justice,' said Sir Thomas. 'You may say what you can in mitigation.'

'Sir, I would have testified earlier that Mr Godwin's death was not caused by the prisoner, but by poison administered by Godwin's own cousin, Sir James Freke, who ought to be here to answer the charge, but he has fled to join the Cavaliers at Wareham. I submit to you, sir, that the accusation of witchcraft against the prisoner arose because ignorant people thought he had caused Mr Godwin's death.'

At this I heard the minister, Mr Lawrence, protesting, but I carried on:

'Sir, if (as I maintain) the murder was done by someone else, this charge against the prisoner ought not to stand. That leaves the charge of witchcraft, but the evidence for that is very doubtful. So he has warts or pimples on his body! why, half the people here must be witches by such proofs! So he talked to his cat! And so do many lonely old people in this town. He divined for water with a hazel twig—so do many who have the gift, which is a good gift from God and nothing to do with the devil.'

Here Sir Thomas interrupted me.

''Fore God,' he said, 'you are not here to review the evidence. This man has been found guilty, and I am allowing you to speak of his character and make a plea for mitigation.'

'With respect, sir,' I said, 'the weakness of the evidence against him is part of my plea. But also he has used his gifts for good. For example, when Mr Whittle here had all his money stolen by Prince Maurice's soldiers, who then hid it where it would never have been found, Malachy Moore out of the goodness of his heart used his God-given art to find it, so that it could be restored to Mr Whittle.'

To his credit Mr Whittle nodded and said:

'Yes, 'tis true, I had lost all my savings, but Mr Moore got them back, including my daughter's dowry.'

'So, sir,' I went on, 'I submit to you that the evidence is very slight, and the character of the prisoner is good, and so I make as strong a plea as I can to you to exercise mercy.'

Sir Thomas stared at me for a moment, frowning and wide-eyed.

'You are a brave man, Mr Apothecary,' he said at last, 'speaking up on behalf of a man accused of such crimes as this man has been found guilty of. But even the good you say he did was, by your own admission, done by supernatural means, and does but strengthen the case against him. As for this other man you say murdered Mr

Godwin, we have no knowledge of him, and can take no notice of your wild accusations. Beware of the devil, Mr Apothecary, for he is subtle and may deceive even the Elect by appearing to do good in order to destroy our souls. Therefore I advise you to look to yourself, and examine yourself lest you also be tainted with the filth of witchcraft and the dreadful wiles of Satan.

'As for the prisoner's character, the testimony of his minister has shown that he has long been looked upon with suspicion as one who has dabbled in forbidden things. I take a very grave view of such things, which no Christian should have anything to do with.

'The prisoner has been found guilty, and must suffer the penalty of the law. A case of this seriousness would normally be reserved for the judges at the Assizes, but in times like these we have to administer justice as best we can. This case is of peculiar wickedness, in that not only has a man's life been taken, against the laws of God and man, but the damnable evil of witchcraft has been practised in our midst. Nothing but the severest punishment will be fitting to root out such evil. I therefore pronounce judgement as follows: the prisoner shall be taken from this place back to prison, and from thence he shall be taken to the special place of execution, namely Maumbury Rings, and there he shall be burned until he is dead, and may the Lord have mercy on his soul.'

The justices rose and filed out, and Malachy was hustled away by the gaol-keeper and a couple of constables. The crowd slowly went out too, and I noticed that some of my acquaintances seemed careful to avoid me, though Joel and one or two others came up and shook my hand and murmured things like 'miscarriage of justice', 'severe sentence', and 'well spoken'.

As I was walking home someone ran up behind me and touched my arm. I turned and saw Rachel Haggard.

'You were there, Mr Judd,' she said. 'I couldn't bear to be, even if I could have got in. But I've heard he's been condemned. Is there nothing to be done?'

'I fear not,' I said.

'But such a dreadful sentence! I can hardly believe that Christians can do such things to one another.'

'Alas, these present wars show all too clearly what they can do. And of course they don't think Malachy is a fellow-Christian, but a witch, a child of Satan.'

'But we know he's not. Couldn't we plead for mercy?'

'The only possible mercy might be for him to be strangled before they burn him. I will try to see Sir Thomas and get him to consent to that.'

'I think it's terrible, horrible!' she said as we reached my shop, and when we told Matthew he too was horrified. They went away hand in hand, their shared sadness making them careless of who might see them.

The sentence was popular in the town though. The prospect of witnessing the burning of a witch at Maumbury Rings excited the more unfeeling part of the populace. The execution was to take place next day. There seemed little more that I could do, except (as I had promised) to appeal for some slight measure of mercy .

So that evening I walked out to Wolfeton in the hope of approaching Sir Thomas though Lady Alicia.

At the gateway I called out, 'What ho! Anyone here?' and the gate-keeper looked out.

'Ar, Mr Judd,' he said (for he knew me from previous visits), 'if you be hoping to see Lady Alicia you'll be disappointed.'

'How is that?'

'She's gone on along back to Hampshire. Her father's come home, I b'lieve, and sent a letter asking her to go to him. The messenger came yesterday, and she left this morning.'

'I'm sorry to miss her, for I hoped she would speak to Sir Thomas for me. But perhaps I can see him myself. Would you send in and ask if he will see me?'

'I doubt if he will. He came back tired after the court sitting. 'Twere a worrying case, by all accounts, an' he weren't in the best of tempers.'

'Well at least let me try to see him. Will you send, or shall I go on to the house?'

'Go on up—you'll find his man Digben in the hall. You can ask him.'

So I went through the courtyard and entered the hall, where a fire was burning and several servants were seated on a bench at the long table enjoying a jug of ale. Digben, Sir Thomas's personal servant, was there, so I asked him to see whether Sir Thomas would allow me to speak with him. He went up the stairs while I stood by the fire waiting. When he returned he was shaking his head.

'I'm sorry, sir, but Sir Thomas is seeing no-one tonight. He has had a tiring day.'

This was not at all favourable, but having come so far I could not give up. I tore a page from the little notebook I carry, and wrote in pencil:

Sir Thomas, Honoured Sir, I have a very important matter to see you about, and beg for no more than five minutes of your time.

I signed the note, addressed it to 'Sir Thomas Trenchard, Kt.', and asked Digben to take it to his master.

He went reluctantly, and I heard him muttering, ''Twill do no good,' but after a little he came back and beckoned me.

'He says you can see him, but not for more than five minutes, mind.'

He led the way up to where Sir Thomas was sitting in an easy chair with his boots off and a glass of wine on a low table beside him.

'Ha, Mr Judd the apothecary!' he exclaimed. 'Have you not said more than enough back there in court? I had a good mind to fine you for contempt.'

'Sir Thomas, I come to you humbly, not to argue more, but simply as a Christian. I know there is nothing more I can do to save the old man, Malachy, from death, now that he's been condemned. What I do ask though, sir, is that you may at least be merciful enough to let him be strangled before he is burned.'

'And why should I do that? The man is a notorious witch.'

'For your own honour, sir, as a Christian man, whose greater glory will come from showing mercy rather than the full rigour of the law.'

'As a Christian man I would remind you, Mr Judd, that the Bible commands us that witches and those who have familiar spirits must be put to death. And it seems to me that burning—a foretaste in fact of the fires of hell which such people must suffer—is very fitting for such evil-doers.'

'Yet the Bible commanded that such should be stoned, not burned,' I said, remembering a sermon of our Dorchester minister, Mr White, on the subject. 'And did not our Lord Himself when faced with an evil-doer say, "Let him that is without sin cast the first stone". So let me still plead with you, sir, to show mercy.'

'You are a good advocate, Mr Judd, but in a bad cause. If this man had simply practised witchcraft I might have consented to do as you ask, but then he used his devilish powers to commit a foul murder. Nothing but the severest punishment can fit such crimes. And let me warn you, Mr Judd, to have a care what you do. You lay yourself open to grave suspicion if you speak up for those who practise witchcraft.'

'I have nothing to do with witchcraft!' I exclaimed with some heat, 'and I challenge anyone to say otherwise. Yet I do beg you sir, to think further on this case tonight. When you have slept and rise tomorrow, please remember mercy, I beseech you sir,'

'I have no more to say. You must leave me. Digben!' he called, and as the manservant came forward, 'show this gentleman out, and don't admit anyone else.'

So I had failed to gain even this small mercy for Malachy, and sadly walked back to Dorchester.

Although by then I too was tired, I could not rest without going once more to the prison, where the keeper (for a tip) allowed me in.

'Here, you'll need a light,' he said, and let me take his lantern.

Even so it was hard to see Malachy in the dark cell or dungeon. He was alone there, sitting not on the bench but on the floor on some straw in the corner. He seemed withdrawn, as if he was hardly aware of his surroundings.

'Is there anything I can do for you?' I asked.

'No zur, thank 'ee zur. I be quite comfortable, thank 'ee.'

'Are you prepared for tomorrow? Do you want to see a minister?'

'No zur, thank 'ee, zur. I be quite comfortable,' he repeated, and I wondered whether he understood what was going to be done to him on the morrow.

I stood for a little, looking at him, waiting for him to speak again. But as he seemed to sink more into himself and to be no longer aware of my presence, I tiptoed away. What could I say? for I had no comfort for him.

Even the gaol-keeper spoke quite kindly of him.

'He's no trouble, even if he is a witch,' he said. 'I'll see he gets a good breakfast, though 'twill be over-cooked afore long!'

His grim joke sickened me, and I went home burdened with the horror of what was to happen in the morning.

Chapter 14 How things ended

THE MORROW, Thursday, July 11th, dawned misty, with the prospect of a sunny day; far too sweet a morning for the horrid things to come.

The townspeople were astir early, and soon many of them were making their way towards the Roman amphitheatre, Maumbury Rings. Some say it is even more ancient than the Romans, and is the work of our ancient British ancestors, or even of giants of long ago. Whatever their origin the Rings are of great use for the people whenever there is need for a large assembly, particularly as today when the gathering was to witness a popular execution. The Rings consist of high earth banks, sloped so that people can sit on them—there is room for several thousand spectators—in a rough circle. An entrance cuts through the bank on the town-ward side, and there is a flat grassy area in the middle.

Much work had been done in the last year or two, when we were expecting to resist a siege, to adapt this ancient place as a fort to guard the approach to the town from the south. Platforms for cannon had been levelled near the top of the bank and a small outwork formed at the side away from the entrance. But since the Royalist army under Lord Carnarvon and Prince Maurice had come, and we had surrendered without a fight, the fortifications at the Rings had largely been neglected

I had wondered whether to stay away, but felt I must see this sad affair through to the very end, so I again left Matthew to mind the shop, and walked up to South Street, where I joined the considerable crowd shuffling along towards the South Gate. Because of the crush of people we could only move slowly, but most were good-tempered, and in fact there was quite a holiday feeling in the air which ill-assorted with my sadness and the terrible scene we were coming to witness, and made me feel more than ever out of place. But I could not turn back now, and was carried along by the crowd, out of the Gate and the quarter mile or so beyond, to where the high green banks of the arena reared up on our left.

We pressed through the nearest entrance, and I found a place to sit high up on the left hand bank and looked around. A tall stake or post had been set up in the centre of the flat area, and some workmen were unloading faggots from a cart and piling them round the stake. They hadn't finished before another cart came through from the town laden with tar-barrels, and these were laid among the faggots.

Soon the grassy banks all round were covered with people, and I was saddened to see even some quite young children had been brought by their parents to watch the horrible show. Friends were waving to each other, calling and smiling. Two or three enterprising traders were going around selling drinks and pies and buns. The feeling of a holiday or a fair seemed to grow ever stronger as we waited, and the noise of talk and laughter grew louder by the minute.

At about nine o' clock a procession arrived: the justices' Clerk of the Peace followed by Sir Thomas and the other two justices, a squad of soldiers with muskets, a cart carrying Malachy with his hands tied, and accompanied by the gaol-keeper and a minister who was exhorting the prisoner. No doubt the minister was urging him to confess and repent, but Malachy appeared not to hear him and sat perfectly still (apart from the jolting of the cart) staring fixedly at his feet. Finally, walking at the rear, came a man in a black mask, carrying a lighted lantern.

The crowd cheered and booed as Malachy came into view, but gradually fell silent as the procession went slowly across and drew near to the centre of the arena, until the cart stopped beside the pyre. Malachy was helped down by the gaol-keeper and then made to climb the pile of faggots by the keeper and a soldier who each took hold of one of his arms. Half way up he stumbled and had to be hauled to his feet by the others. At the top they turned him round and thrust his back against the stake and fixed him there with a rusty chain round his waist, and then the gaol-keeper and the soldier jumped down. There was an expectant hush, with not a murmur from all the great crowd.

Then the Clerk of the Peace stepped forward and read the sentence again. Most of the spectators could not hear him, but they no doubt understood the gist of what he was saying. When he had finished the crowd stirred, as if there was a universal drawing of breath. Then the minister stepped forward and made a long prayer, raising his hands and eyes to heaven in a most fervent manner, though again most of us could not hear his words. I think however that he was beseeching the Lord to protect us from the devil and that the aweful fate of the condemned man might warn others of the dangers of becoming enmeshed in Satan's wiles.

At last he was done, and at a nod from Sir Thomas the man with the lighted lantern, who had been standing to one side, used it to kindle a torch and, when it was burning well, approached the pile to set it alight. Again the crowd fell absolutely silent. There was not a cough or a whisper as everyone was held in dreadful expectation.

All at once the silence was broken by a disturbance from the town end of the amphitheatre as a man came running in shouting 'Help! help! The enemy are upon us! Come back inside the walls!'

The man with the flaming torch paused with it poised at the edge of the pile. The shouting man ran up to Sir Thomas and spoke rapidly to him. Sir Thomas raised his voice so that the people could hear.

'Soldiers are approaching on the other side of the town,' he announced. 'Let there be no panic, but make your way back inside the walls. Let the guards go to their posts. These proceedings are postponed. Take the prisoner back to gaol.'

'No panic,' he said, but there was a stampede to leave. It was a wonder that no one was hurt in the rush. Malachy was taken down and put back in the cart and taken away by the gaol-keeper, and I followed in the crowd. There was a terrible crush as we squeezed out of the entrance, and I was relieved when I found myself outside the Rings without mishap. If anyone had fallen they would surely have died, trampled under foot. But once I was out of the narrow place it was easier, and I hurried with the rest back along the road to South Gate. Again there was a crush as we struggled to get through into the safety of the town, though the guards at the gate did their best to control the crowd and tried in vain to make the people enter in an orderly fashion. It was fortunate that the enemy had not attacked on this side of the town.

As a member of the militia I went at once to see if I were needed. We were still unclear as to who the approaching soldiers were, whether Cavaliers or Roundheads, or even some group of free-lances. Nor was it certain that we would (or should) bar the gates to them. Mostly we seemed to find it best to allow armies from either side to come in unresisted, and hope that they would not do too much damage.

But this time the decision whether to resist or not had been taken from us—and by women! As I reached the far end of South Street, at Cornhill, I could hear a lot of shouting, and the occasional shot of musket or pistol, and women screaming. It seemed that an assault was being made at the lower end of town, by or outside East Gate.

I reached the Gate and found it was still open, though armed men stood by ready to swing the great doors to if it should be necessary. But the fighting seemed to be a little way off still, so I rushed through, and soon realised that it was apparently happening in Fordington, the parish just outside the town walls, which in all but name is a suburb of Dorchester, and stretches up a hill from the river and the water-meadows to the fine big church with its tall tower. At the lower end, all around the Pound near the high road to Blandford, and up the hill among the houses, there were horsemen turning this way and that. Barriers had been put across the streets—bits of furniture, tree branches, ropes and the like—which impeded their movements, and a lot of people, many of them women, were darting out from among the houses and throwing things at the soldiers.

My first thought was relief that the fighting was still outside the town, and that Agnes was no longer out there with her parents in Fordington. But then I felt anxious for them, and hoped they were securely barricaded in their house. Provided they stayed indoors I trusted that they would be safe.

The attackers had obviously been surprised to encounter such resistance, and seemed to be milling about in some confusion. From the look of them I guessed they were Cavaliers, and someone said that they had come from Wareham. Their leader, whom I afterwards discovered was the redoubtable Colonel O'Brien, the Royalist commander of that town, was trying to rally them, and lead them out of Fordington and into Dorchester. But the women in particular fought like tigers, or rather tigresses, and kept goading the horsemen to turn and turn about, for they did not know from which direction the next shower of missiles would come. Prominent among the women was one in a blue head-scarf. She was throwing stones with great accuracy—I saw her nearly knock a trooper off his horse—and she was shouting encouragements to her companions and abuse at the enemy. Then I realised who it was—Rachel Haggard—and there beside her was Matthew Barton, who had evidently abandoned my shop to throw himself into the fray.

It took only a moment for me to see all this, and it seemed obvious that the efforts of the women could only delay the inevitable attack on Dorchester itself, so the most useful thing I could do would be to get back inside the Gate and help to resist the assault when it came. As I turned to do so I saw Matthew's father, Mr Edward Barton, standing nearby. He was clapping his hands and shouting encouragements to his son, though Matthew could not possible have heard him: 'Oh very well done! Up an' at 'em! Let 'em have it! Oh, good shot, sir! Halloo, halloo, halloo!'

'Do you see who's beside your Matthew?' I called to him.

'I do! I do! She is magnificent! Give it to 'em! Halloo, halloo!'

And then to my amazement I saw Rachel's father, Mr Haggard, was also looking on. I would have expected him to welcome a Cavalier victory. But no, his Dorchester feelings got the better of his Royalist principles—or maybe it was the sight of his daughter so recklessly showering missiles on the troops. At anyrate, he was cheering and shouting encouragement as enthusiastically as his enemy, Mr Barton.

He became aware of who it was cheering beside him, and he and Barton exchanged a look. I could not say it was friendly; more perhaps of surprise and a certain wary respect. Yet they did not speak to each other, but turned back to watch and cheer.

I went then to take up a position inside the Gate. Our being outside the town when the enemy approached meant that we had not had time to form up in proper units, and all I had for weapon was a cudgel. But our blood was up, and we were determined that this time Dorchester would not give in without a fight. Also we were challenged and inspired by the example of the women, whose courage amazed us.

Those like Rachel who were fighting in Fordington were now cut off from the town. A few slipped in through the Gate before we closed it, and the rest retreated behind the Fordington houses. I was relieved to see that the Cavaliers did not seem eager to carry on the fight in that area, no doubt fearing to get entangled in the back alleys where their foes would have the advantage, but came storming up to the Gate.

'Open up in the name of the King, you rebels!' roared Colonel O'Brien.

In answer we jeered at him from the wall, and someone fired a musket at him, but missed. The Cavaliers came on, pressing against the Gate, and suddenly it gave way. In our haste it must have been insecurely fastened.

Now began a really desperate struggle. Some of the horsemen pushed though and began slashing about with their long swords.

Others dismounted and engaged in hand-to-hand struggles just inside the Gate.

Barriers made of carts, hurdles, ladders and anything else to hand, had been hastily thrown across the street to prevent them rushing up through the town, and in addition two chains had been stretched across a little way up from the gate. They had been placed in readiness for this very purpose the previous year, but never before used, and had been fixed across while I was watching the fight in Fordington.

In spite of this and our resolute resistance, I fear we would have been vanquished, with what bloody consequences for us all I dread to think, if help had not come speedily. But come it did thanks to the quick thinking of the Mayor. For as soon as he heard of the imminent attack he had had the wit to send a swift rider over the hill to Weymouth to seek help from the Roundhead garrison. By good fortune the messenger had met Major Thomas Sydenham (one of the formidable family of brothers, all of whom fought for Parliament) already armed and leading a troop of horse out of Melcombe. As soon as they heard they were needed they spurred their horses and came sweeping over the hill in the nick of time.

They galloped round outside the walls and took the Cavaliers in the rear. There was a short sharp fight around the Gate, and then the enemy broke and began galloping back the way they had come, pursued by Major Sydenham and his men. They chased them all the way to Wareham and captured about 160 out of the 240 or so who had set out with Colonel O'Brien. Eight of the prisoners were Irish, so hated and feared over here in England that Major Sydenham had seven of them hanged at once. The eighth was spared because he hanged the others.

We heard all about this later, of course. Our immediate task was to tend the wounded and bury the dead. It was really surprising how, after such a fierce fight, so few were wounded or killed; but my skills were soon much in use amongst those who needed them. I saw Matthew coming in, hand in hand with Rachel, and Mr Barton just behind them smiling all over his face. 'There's a big change,' I thought, 'and a marriage can't be far off.'

But I needed help, so asked Matthew to fetch bandages and ointments from my shop. Rachel stayed among the wounded, trying to bring them what comfort she could. Presently Matthew came back with supplies and helped me bind up wounds and fetch things as I needed them. Doctors and surgeons from the town were also doing their part, and together we soon had most of the wounded men (and a few women) attended to.

I was beginning to think that we had done all we could when Matthew touched my arm.

'There's a Cavalier officer—his wounds have been bandaged, but I think he's dying and he wants help.'

I followed him to just outside the Gate where, at the side of the road, the officer was lying. I knelt beside him.

'I'm going,' he whispered. 'I need a priest.'

'Are you a Catholic?' I asked.

'No, Church of England—but any minister will do. I must unburden my conscience.'

The minister who had been at Maumbury Rings was saying a prayer over a man across the road, so I rose and asked him to come. He knelt beside the officer and took his hand.

'Help me sit up,' whispered the officer, so I knelt on the other side and supported him.

'I must unburden myself before I die,' he said. 'I have a murder on my conscience, and an innocent man may have died for it.'

'What is your name?' asked the minister.

'Freke, Sir James Freke. I discovered my cousin, George Godwin, was planning to give Weymouth into the hands of the Roundheads, so I poisoned him. The blame was laid upon an old man, Malachy Moore, who I fear has died for it.'

'Not yet,' I said, 'your confession may be just in time to save him.'

'I'm glad of it,' he whispered. 'Good, good.' Then he coughed up blood and, with a sudden paroxysm, he died.

The minister said a short prayer over Sir James, then got up to leave, but I grasped his arm.

'Sir,' I said, 'you were at the execution this morning, and have now heard the truth. Will you come with me and testify to the justices, and have Malachy Moore released?'

'He was accused of witchcraft as well as murder,' he said sourly.

'But if he had not been suspected of murder he would never have been accused of witchcraft,' I said. 'At the very least it is our duty to inform the justices what this man confessed.'

He did agree to that, and so, as my work for the wounded was done, I went with him in search of Sir Thomas. We could not find him, but one of his fellow justices, Sir Richard Strode, was near the Cornmarket talking to the Mayor, congratulating him on his prompt action which had saved the town.

'Sir,' I said, going up to him, this minister and I have heard a confession which you ought to be told about.'

'Aren't you the fellow who tried to defend the witch?' he asked.

'Yes, and it would have been well if I had been listened to, sir,' I said. 'But you will, I trust hear what this reverend minister has to say.'

'What is it?'

'Sir Richard,' said the minister, 'I have just attended one of the Cavaliers. He was badly wounded and died soon after I reached him, but almost with his last breath he wished to make confession of a grievous sin. He told me that his name was Sir James Freke and that he had killed his cousin, George Godwin, by poison. He said it was on his conscience that an innocent man had been blamed, and might have wrongfully suffered death for it.'

'And that innocent man is the one you were about to burn today, Malachy Moore,' I said.

'Can this be true?' said Sir Richard.

'Indeed sir,' I said, 'I too heard Sir James confess. And that only confirmed what I was told long ago by a Cavalier soldier who had heard him boast about it. He killed his cousin to try to prevent the rising against the Royalist garrison in Weymouth and the port being handed over to the Earl of Essex, although as we know the murder made no difference. The blame was put upon Mr Moore by the blind prejudice of the village people, who when they saw a sudden and unusual death attributed it to witchcraft, and Sir James did nothing to save him from them. But now Mr Moore ought to be released.'

'He was found guilty of witchcraft as well as of murder,' said the minister again.

'But the witchcraft charge arose from the murder,' I said, 'they were linked, and if he is innocent of the one, so he is of the other. Undoubtedly, sir, he is innocent.'

'By heaven, I think you're right,' said Sir Richard. 'I had my doubts about the verdict, especially when that rogue Richard Still gave evidence. Moore had better be freed.'

'Can you give the order, sir?' I asked.

'It's irregular, but so are these times, so why not? But you'd better get him away somewhere privately, while the people have something else to think about.'

'Please would you write an order for his release for me to show to the gaol-keeper?'

He went into a stationer's shop nearby, and asked for ink and paper. He wrote: *To the Keeper of Dorchester Gaol: The prisoner named Malachy Moore is to be released forthwith. Richard Strode, Kt., Examining Magistrate.* He handed it to me with a smile, and when I had thanked him I took it straight along to the prison.

The Keeper seemed rather put out.

'By the Lord,' he said, 'I do wish the justices would make up their minds. The people won't like it. They'd set their hearts on a good burning.'

'They've had a good battle instead,' I said, 'so now, let's have Mr Moore set free and out of the way.'

'Well, if there's a riot the magistrates will have to see to it,' he said shrugging his shoulders, and led me along the passage and opened the heavy door.

'They've come for you,' he said.

Malachy was sitting as usual, hunched up against the wall. He looked like a hunted hare.

'It's all right, Malachy,' I said. 'I've come to take you away. You're free.'

'I daun' understan',' he said. 'Am I not to be burned?'

'No, you are free. Sir James Freke is dead, but just before he died he confessed. He killed Mr Godwin, as I told you, and you are innocent. So come along, get up and let's leave.'

I seized his arm and helped him to his feet and led him along the passage. Once he tripped on a rough paving-stone and I had to hold him tight to prevent him falling. At the outer door I made him pause while I looked up and down to see that it was safe to take him into the street, but although there were people about their attention was still fixed on the area around the East Gate, where men were clearing up the relics of the battle or helping some of the wounded to walk away. I led Malachy out and, trying to keep myself between him and the people we met, took him as fast as he could go away from the High Street.

I wanted to get him out of the town as soon as possible, in case people started to cry for his death as a witch again. But what to do with him was a puzzle. He could not go back to his home in Upwey, that was certain, for the people there, including the parson, were still so prejudiced against him and would think he was in league with the Evil One, and might ill-treat or even kill him. I wondered whether I could ask my uncle and aunt in Portesham to care for him for a little, until some provision could be made for him.

At all events I would take him to my shop while I decided what to do, so I led him by back ways to Durn Lane. We had nearly reached my door when I saw Jacob Perrin, the smuggler. He greeted me warmly.

'Micah! Just the man I hoped to see!'

'How comes it that you're here, Jacob?' I asked.

'I happened to have some business in the town, an' was sorry to find everyone seemed to have gone to see the burning, including the fellow I had come to meet. So I was in the King's Arms havin' a drink while I decided whether to go home or wait, when this fighting started. I kept my head indoors like the brave fellow I am, but when all was quiet I ventured out. "I wonder if Micah Judd was in the thick o' that?" I wondered, an' was jus' coming along to see that you were all right.'

'Yes indeed, Jacob,' I said. 'I'm fine, thank you. But I've a problem on my hands.'

I explained to him who it was I had with me, and how although Malachy was innocent he would be unsafe in Upwey, especially as Mr Lawrence, the vicar there, was so against him, and I needed to find somewhere for him to go for a few days.

Perrin had looked rather doubtful until that point, for he could see that I was going to ask him to shelter the old man while I made arrangements for a settled home for him. And I could not really blame Jacob, because taking care of a man who had been accused of witchcraft, even though he had been declared not guilty, could put his helper in danger. But the mention of Mr Lawrence made him change.

'By the Lord, I know that minister,' he said, 'an' a crabbed cantankerous fellow he is. He's tried to harass me more than once, and threatened to haul me before the justices. I wouldn' trust him further than I could throw a bull by the tail! Let me think, now, and I may be able to help.'

We went into my shop, and I sat him and Malachy down while I fetched them each a mug of ale, and also assured Agnes of my safety. When I came back I found Perrin had got Malachy to talk a little.

'Well, granfer, do you want to go back to Upwey?' he was asking.

'No zur,' said Malachy, 'now my ol' Simmany's dead I don't

care for that pleace no more.'

'How about coming with me?' said Perrin, and looking at me he said, 'You know, I've got room at my farm, an' I could do with someone to keep an eye on it when I'm away, an' feed the hens an' collect the eggs and so on. How about that, granfer? Would you care to try coming along o' me?'

'That I would, zur, if it wouldn' be too much trouble.'

'I've left my cart down at the King's Arms,' said Perrin. 'I'll go an' fetch it, an' we can be on our way.' He brushed aside my thanks and went off, and soon I was waving good-bye as Malachy rode away. How long he would be able to stay at the farm I did not know, but Perrin said I need not hurry to make other arrangements.

Malachy had escaped just in time, for the gaol-keeper was right. When the townsfolk recovered from the shock of the fight, their thoughts turned to witch-burning again, and when they realised the victim had disappeared some of them were angry. I don't know what Sir Thomas Trenchard thought of it, but Sir Richard Strode must have persuaded him to make no fuss, and I made sure that Sir James's confession was made known all around the town, so in the end most decent folk agreed that a great injustice had been prevented. One or two asked me what had happened to Malachy, and I told them he had gone away—I thought it safest not to say where, though I told Matthew and no doubt he told Rachel.

One result that particularly pleased me was that my relationship with Agnes's parents were much improved and we were almost back on our old good footing. Her mother said she was sorry to have doubted me, and her father went so far as to praise my 'steadfastness' (as he called it) in sticking up for Malachy.

Another result of the fight was also very welcome. On the following Monday morning I noticed that Matthew came to work in a joyous mood. He came into the shop whistling, and as he washed bottles he was humming under his breath.

'What's come over you, Matthew,?' I asked him. 'Anyone would think you had found a pot of gold!'

'Oh but I have,' he said. 'After seeing Rachel throwing stones at the Cavaliers Father has quite altered his opinion of her. He says she ought to be named after Deborah or Jael, or any of those other great women of the Bible.'

'What does her father think?'

'He professes to be shocked at what she did, but I think really he is proud of her. At all events he is not forbidding her to speak to me.'

'And is she doing that?'

He smiled and wiped hard at a phial.

'Yes,' he said.

'It seems to me that you'll have mind your manners, if you share bed and board with such a fierce Amazon! When is the wedding to be?'

'Oh, we haven't got that far. We're not even officially betrothed. I fear her father and mine will never see eye to eye about religion or King and Parliament, but perhaps now they'll be more friendly to each other.'

'Not curse each other in the public street?' I suggested with a smile.

'Never again, I hope. So I think they won't object to our proper betrothal.'

'So when it that to take place?'

'As soon as we can get the parents to agree on a date. And we'd like you to be present, Mr Judd, as you've been such a help to us.'

In fact it was little more than a fortnight later that Agnes and I attended the betrothal ceremony, though the wedding itself would not be for a number of months yet.

But I must end this narrative with a visit I made to Monkton to see how Malachy was doing at Jacob Perrin's. One evening I rode out of South Gate and along the familiar Weymouth road, and turned right towards his dilapidated farm.

As I clattered into his yard Perrin looked out from the stable.

'Hey, Micah,' he said, 'have you come to see if I've been bewitched?'

'I was certainly wondering how you were getting along with old Malachy. Is all well? Is he proving a satisfactory guest?'

'Oh yes indeed, he's no trouble at all. I can't see what folk had against him. But I reckon they followed the lead o' that Rector of Upwey—a bigoted jobbernowl, I call him!'

I laughed at this description of that dignified and self-satisfied cleric.

'Well, Malachy's safely beyond his reach,' I said. 'Is he able to help you at all around the farm?'

'Aye, surely. He's been going round the meadow with his hazel rod, telling me where I can dig for water, and he's feedin' the hens and lookin' after the place when I'm away, as I hoped he would. An' Micah, you need not bother to find somewhere else for him to live. He can stay here.'

'Jacob, thank you,' I shook his hand. 'You are a good friend and a good man.'

'No, you musn' call me that; I'm a wicked fellow, a smuggler! But I'm glad to have the old fellow about the place.'

'And how is he? what's his state of mind, after all he's been through?'

'Well, 'tis remarkable really. I thought he'd mayhap be more disturbed after all that, what with being dragged to prison and nearly being burned. But though he often sits quiet, as if his thoughts are far away, he seems calm enough.'

'I'm glad to hear that, for I was worried that being treated as a witch might send him mad. Is he about? Can I see him?'

'Aye, you'll find him up at the house wi' his new friend.'

'New friend?' I said. 'Who's that?'

'You go an' meet him,' said Perrin, and went back inside the stable chuckling.

So I went over to the house, and sure enough there was old Malachy sitting by the door on a bench in the sun—and on his lap was a black kitten with a white face.

I sat down beside him and asked how he was getting on.

'This be a good pleace, zur,' he said, 'an' Mairster Perrin be a good man. So thank 'ee, zur, for all you've done for me.'

'Oh, don't mention it, Malachy. I'm so glad you've found a peaceful spot after all the dreadful time you've had. And you've got a new friend, I see,' I said, stroking the kitten. 'what are you going to call him?'

Malachy looked abashed and I do believe he even blushed.

'Well, I hope you don't mind, zur,' he said, and paused.

'Go on,' I said.

'Well, beggin' your pardon, zur, I thought to call him after you—"Mr Judd", zur, to remember you by.'

I smiled and stroked the kitten's back, and a rumbling purr came out. Things had 'come around' all right at last.

For those who like to know the history

Although the stories of Malachy Moore, Rachel and Matthew, and Lady Alicia are fiction, the movements of the armies happened much as described. Plotters in Melcombe and Weymouth did invite the Earl of Essex to come, and handed over the towns to him when they had overcome the Cavalier garrison. Also Lord Hopton tried to conscript Dorchester men into his army, but they all escaped. Colonel O'Brien came from Wareham to attack Dorchester, and was held off mainly by the women until Major Sydenham galloped up and routed him.